THE MAID'S REQUEST

MICHÈLE DESBORDES

The Maid's Request

A story

Translated from the French by
Shaun Whiteside

faber and faber

First published in France in 1998
by Éditions Verdier
First published in Britain in 2003
by Faber and Faber Limited
3 Queen Square, London WCIN 3AU

Typeset by Faber and Faber Limited
Printed in England by Clays Ltd, St Ives plc

© Éditions Verdier, 1998
Translation © Shaun Whiteside 2003

The right of Shaun Whiteside to be identified as translator
of this work has been asserted in accordance with Section 77 of the
Copyright, Designs and Patents Act 1988

A CIP record for this book
is available from the British Library

ISBN 0–571–21006–6

2 4 6 8 10 9 7 5 3 1

He knew that her name was Tassine and that she was a native of the region, he couldn't have guessed her age, let alone said whether or not she was pretty, he looked at her attentively with the air of being elsewhere; he looked at her without seeing her, that was what she thought in the end, and then she saw his face growing animated, a vague smile appearing on his lips. A movement towards her. Whether it was interest or simple courtesy she couldn't have said. Then she smiled in turn.

The wind rose and a cloud passed before the sun, darkening the cliffs, the green of the great yews. With a slow gesture she showed the garden and the house, then walked ahead of him up the grand staircase. That was all that day in Clan Manor and he was tired from the long journey.

THE LAST COUNTRY

*T*hey had arrived via the slopes, along the road that joined the river after the last villages and the vines. From a long way off they had seen the grey roofs and the crest of the cliffs and, down below among the willows, fishermen in a little boat. Coming along the paths and through the small wood they had flanked the river; they walked slowly, leading their horses; they looked at the clear water, almost blue in the sun, and on the other side of the river the vast plain. It was a Sunday morning and the bells were ringing, joyful in the April sky, in the cool wind that drove the clouds towards the sea. Villagers were leading their animals down to the shore. Behind them, towards the Sologne, they heard the baying of a pack of hounds.

There were five of them on their horses, the youngest barely twenty with curls to his shoulders, the oldest age-less, perhaps an old man, whose beauty still held the eye; pale eyes in a weather-beaten face, his body straight and slender beneath the brown woollen pelisse. Anyone *observing them would have known they had been on a long journey; their faces were marked by weariness and perhaps a certain unease, the confusion of strangers who have come from a long way away.*

Soon they stopped and looked at the countryside around them; after the forest it seemed vast, like the sky above the slopes and on the other side of the river towards the plains – with a broad gesture the old man silently showed them – perhaps they were thinking of the Lombardy plain and the colours of the sky at evening over the Po; this was not a time for words, they were silent, the pupils and the manservant, waiting on the horses; the old man understood, he himself had nothing to say and would say nothing, not even of the weariness or the difficult days they had just been through, that long road into exile, the seventy-three days they had spent on their horses in the rain and the cold of the mountains.

They had waited for the worst of the winter to pass and put off leaving till February, without an escort or a coach as far as Lyons; that was how he had decided to do it. That year a freezing wind had blown from the peaks. For the first few days, from Milan to the Mont-Genevre pass, they had been filled with courage and despite their apprehension they had been in a hurray to reach the mountains, he probably more than the others. It was before the great rains came; they led the horses at a jog; in the inns at evening they consorted with the muleteers as they loosened the girths and walked the exhausted animals, washed their muzzles and chests; happy to have reached their staging post they laughed some more and lingered in the courtyards before sitting down at table with merchants and pilgrims, with servants leading the masters' horses to Turin and Geneva; they talked about the peaks and the endless winter, of difficult roads and exhausted animals, of the women of Milan, the most beautiful in Italy.

Soon it had rained for three weeks solid and the horses had grown tired, refusing to drink or eat; the men observed their swollen lids and sad eyes, put salt in the first helping of oats and washed their overheated muzzles with vinegar; they watched the horses, anxiously waiting for the moment when they would stamp their feet and sniff the ground with their nostrils; everything was a potential danger and sometimes it seemed as though death was on the prowl, watching men and animals and the world around them. Sadness was always there, even if on some days the sweetness of the air or the blue of the sky told a different story. They were leaving their country with him, for how long they did not know; the old man said he would not be coming back, that he would die among strangers. In the evenings in the inn they sat apart and supped in silence, thinking only of the moment when they would go to sleep, unaware of the wines and the chambermaids; worn out and dirty they climbed the stairs to their bed-chambers with their sheets and blankets, the skins they spread out on the mattresses; they were given the new room, the white room or the St Catherine room; without saying a word or even looking at one another they slumped on the beds.

When two horses had been injured on a rocky path they had had to leave them behind, so they had abandoned the Sicilian that had been theirs for almost seven years and the black horse Borgia had given them; the mules, braver, carried the chests, everything the old man owned in the way of transportable goods, and the three paintings he was never parted from as well as the litter where he would sometimes sit. A few times after the Maurienne valley he gave up mounting his horse; it was cold and he felt wretched.

He would not be coming back, he would not be covering this path again, the seventy-three days in the rain and the cold of the mountains where, when the thunderstorm threatened, they stopped in refuges and sanctuaries, and in the evenings when, lost in fog, they were unable to find anything, they slept under their hastily erected tent on the ground in coats and the silk blankets, when they didn't spend the night waiting for *sleep that refused to come. For seventy-three days they had lived on the horses, thought, suffered, considered the world from the saddle, dismounting only to eat, piss and sleep, or, when their feet were chilled, to walk to warm the blood, never knowing what the next moment would bring, only the rapid and familiar rhythm of courage and fatigue, the misery of feeling the cold and damp of the heights, telling themselves that in the morning, barely rested, they would be setting off again in the rain and fog, that off they would go, off they would go.*

And no doubt yet more misery thinking about the days before and the goodbyes, the faces they would never see again, the cities and hills of Tuscany, most recently seeking each other's eyes then turning away, sometimes even joking and laughing. Leaving and parting were nothing new, they had always had to leave, seek new masters elsewhere; he had travelled Italy on horseback with his pupils, known all the royal courts and everyone the country held to be a lord, painted frescoes for the churches and portraits of the women they loved, devised arcades and columns for the palaces, suits and liveries for their weddings, not to mention cannons and bombards, and fortifications against the enemy when the wars had come; sometimes their protectors died or his own body was exhausted with fever and study, fresh sadness, life

*unravelled. To the point of dizziness, of bitterness —
and yet, when things were at their worst, a foreign
king had called on him, asking him to enter his ser-
vice, first in his court in Milan and then in France,
and each time the king had asked him, he, the
painter-sculptor-architect-engineer, despite the offer
of princely dwellings and incomes, had appeared to
ignore the request, worrying about how well it would
suit his final years, thus stirring the royal desire,
exacerbating it without pride or self-interest, finally
accepting and informing the foreign king, who was
offering an income, a manor and servants, that he
accepted on his own behalf and that of his pupils this
most generous invitation, and would do his best to give
satisfaction.*

*In mid-April the sky had brightened, slashes of rain-
washed blue appearing between the clouds; these alone
had revived their courage, and they had left the
strongholds and the great alpine valleys for the low
country. Day after day they had seen herds emerging
from stables, sometimes a vine appearing on a slope or
mulberry bushes on a mountainside. On their last
evening in the Arve valley they had supped on partridge,
chickens and celery, then apples with biscuits, all washed
down with a local wine that had warmed their blood.
They were half-way through their journey; they had*

joked and forgotten the difficult days, they had talked about the cold and the dizzying paths and the ones who had crossed the mountains with their armies, Hannibal who had come here with soldiers from Africa and elephants used to the sweetness of the savannahs, and how after crossing the icy slopes, exhausted, desperate and unable to see anything of the world around them, the African soldiers had lain down on the ground, one by one they had lain down on the snow. Hard, cold, unknown. They had talked about Frenchmen who had gone to reclaim their crowns from Italy and crossed the mountains on their little horses, barely noticing the ravines over which they threw their bridges, advancing as far as the plains of Saluces with equipment and cannon and courtesans seated on the mules, the girls of the Limousin who would go with them to the end, who would die one after the other of the soldiers' illnesses, sweating beneath their make-up and taffetas dirtied by the long mule-rides, the French outfits in which they had crossed the mountains. It was in June in the Bay of Naples.

They were met in Lyons, fresh horses and the coach sent by the king so he could rest. They were there for Easter and the spring fairs, there was a big crowd and the streets were full of foreigners; he wanted to meet the city's Italians, look for books in the bookshops, but there were so many people and the streets were so dark and muddy that he had soon asked to leave. From the quays of the Saône after the rain they had gazed once again towards Italy, then continued through the mountains, the dark valleys that led to the other river; at Roanne they had looked at the white houses and the flat-bottomed fishing-boats. They were going down to Orléans; they had taken the road through the plains, short days on transverse roads to avoid the wind, and that had held them up too. Near Moulins and Bourges they had reached the Sologne, the lowlands, the forests, ploughed fields and hemp. One evening in Romorantin the sun had appeared and the forest had gently coloured, the trees were sprouting leaves, the light made the vague fringe of the hedges iridescent; for a moment he had forgotten who he was and where he came from, he looked at the new country, approached the unknown.

High mass was drawing to a close. From the bridge on to the island they saw the church emptying, the bells rang even louder, an accompaniment to the sun and the gaiety of the blue sky; they looked at the palace, three men on horseback reaching the terraces from the towers. The castle was spread out on the cliff, galleries and pinnacles, terraces and long avenues; the French wanted to see the beauties of Naples and Florence with their own eyes, wanted them quickly and urgently: at their request castle-builders and gardeners, goldsmiths, stucco-makers and carvers of alabaster had crossed the Alps. While the woods all around had been turned into upper gardens and lower gardens, pergolas and orchards of quince trees and white mulberries, the workmen and the masons by the river had, following the instructions of the Italians, built the loveliest houses ever seen in the country, working every night by candlelight, and in the winter making fires to thaw the stones.

They watched the gleaming water, almost blue beneath the sky, the peaceful river where the kings stopped and ordered their houses built; in summer they saw the sun setting over the sands as pale as a maritime beach, a contented flow in the middle of the country, unimaginable anywhere but here where the scale of things seemed to have been invented to provide order and reassurance, to calm disorder and torment. Villages and towns forgot wars and hard times, the soldiers who, on their little horses, reached Italy, where in the winter by torchlight they entered unknown cities and at evening in the tents succumbed to Naples' fever.

Three knights reached the heights of the palace; they saw them advance on to the ramparts, their caps and hackbuts shining in the sun. He watched Fanfoia, Melzi and Salai, his pupils, and behind them the mules carrying the chests and the paintings, he asked them to set off again for Clan Manor. They passed along the base of the fort and, turning left after the church, they rode through the woods along the top of the cliff. Ringed by pale fog the sun rose above the river, soon behind them; making a long, pale and motionless patch in the sky it reached the spire of the church. It was just eleven o'clock.

THE REQUEST

*T*hey barely saw her as they came in; she was washing in the courtyards, passing back and forth along the walls with buckets and wet cloths, wrung with a twist of the wrist, tiny, dressed all in grey, the only thing that gleamed the white of her hair. She threw water over the paving-stones then set off back for the well while the sun rose in the sky, reaching the tips of the oak trees. She had heard the horses on the road and, as they passed the last houses, the barking of the dogs behind the walls, their voices as they drew closer to the house, foreign and resonant in the pale spring sky. Nearly noon. She had been waiting for them for a long time, waiting every day, in fact; the message had arrived from Lyons and Romorantin, they wouldn't be long, just a matter of days, they would be there for the last Sunday in April. She had washed, dusted, scattered the heather in great armfuls on the ground, organized and planned the task she would have to perform. The manor was not a castle, but still big enough to keep a person busy from dawn till dusk and probably more: kitchen, downstairs bedrooms and upstairs bedrooms, cellar, the gallery in the park and beyond the terraces the stable, sheds and woodshed, wood and coal for the kitchen, kindling for the bedchambers. She had waited quietly and patiently, not even trying to imagine the master who was coming or the ones who were coming with him. She had worked in the houses by the river for more than twenty years.

She saw them passing through the big gate, the pupils and then the old man, then the mules with the chests and the sheets and all the things they were bringing from Italy. For their part, they barely saw her. She crossed the terrace from the direction of the stables, passed along the walls with a bucket in each hand; by the gallery she stopped, put down the buckets and looked at the new arrivals. She looked at the old man and the pupils, the manservant, straightened herself and, brushing back a curl that had fallen from her coif, she came towards them with little steps in grey fustian. The sun fell on the yew trees and the boxwood bushes on the terraces, behind her the sand of the avenues bleached white. She smiled without a word and walked ahead of them into the house.

They looked at the gardens and the terraces, looked at her, passed along the gallery to the bed-chambers and rested. The manservant watered the horses and walked them, holding their reins; later he unloaded the mules, unpacked the master's belongings. The pupils came and joined him, they talked together for a long time.

*B*eneath the trees they listened to the river, dark and cool in the curve of the slope; on windless evenings they heard it rolling over the pebbles, a clear and calming sound. Because of the river and the tall trees, the white cliffs that ran up towards the castle, they said they liked the house. As the sun sank they saw the light on stone making the colour tremble, giving the cliffs a golden glow minute by minute. They stayed in the gardens and on the terraces. Time barely passed. They felt as though they had not finished arriving, had not finished leaving Italy.

She watched them attentively; they caught her eye upon them, not suspicious, her gaze merely curious and apprehensive. She observed the pale-eyed old man; he watched her and smiled without saying a word. He rested and, apart from two or three visits to the Italians in the town and walks along the river, didn't go out much. On sunny days he walked in the park or on the terraces, or ordered a table set up outside; he wrote, looked at the trees in the avenues, drew; the weather was fine, the clouds drifted across the banks, pale and swift, low in the sky. From time to time some pupil or servant would arrive with ink, pens and paper, and then he had them bring out the horses, the jennet, the black horse and the hackney mare. Sitting on the terrace he drew the horses. Later he would come back and rejoin the pupils in the studio, and they would make a woman's portrait or an angel for a chapel in his style; they talked about hands and light, he corrected an outline, a lowered eyelid, lightened a shadow. They said nothing else all through those days, getting used to the new country. Shortly before supper they came down to the kitchen to find her at the big table, peeling cabbages and turnips, vegetables for the following day, chopping onions into a basket. They paid her their compliments and sat round the fire, fell silent for a moment and then started talking among themselves, in a sweet and singing language she didn't understand. She watched them in silence, not even seeming to see them, smiled gently; with a shrug she turned round and looked out of the windows.

A peasant, that's what they had been told, from

the peat bogs, further off beyond the first forest, one of those who served in the houses on the river, who had always served. When they were barely grown they worked on the harvests, with sickles they mowed the hay or the rushes in the ponds, retted the hemp and tended the animals; at evening in the hovels they sewed and wove in silence unless it was winter, when they gathered together, though they were never all that talkative, having learned early to be silent. She was small and frail, like a child, they said to themselves, her face was fine and her nose delicate below her broad forehead, nothing to suggest that she had come from the ponds and the lowlands, those hamlets where well before nightfall farms and hovels and woods all around vanished into the fog, the white mists rising from the ploughed fields, and noises even in the grey light, the depth of night. Her hair must have been fair, perhaps it still was beneath the coif from which there emerged through a pale mist, light and trembling, a curl smoothed on her temple, she was forty, forty-five perhaps, she herself didn't know.

She cooked carp and lamprey for them, under-sized pike from the river, eels that she skinned, turning them inside-out like a glove, she served them melons, figs and lemons like in Italy. At her corner of the table she ate her vegetable or barley soup, her curds, lifting the bowl with one hand and with the other digging with the spoon; she ate silently, not even the chink of spoon against pewter or the sound of the glass that she emptied with tiny sips and put back on the table. If they invited her to join them, she assured them there was no need and they shouldn't worry about her. So she went on as before. When they arrived she was finishing her meal, and when she had finished it she stayed there for a moment, shoulders low and head bowed, motionless for one last second as though they had never been there or as though they in turn had ignored her.

When vespers rang she rose to her feet and laid the table; she went to the dresser, pulled out the table-cloth and with a broad gesture she rolled it out on the table, smoothed it with the back of her hand, put out the glasses and bowls. Her movements were precise and measured, her eyes lowered and the silence suggested application and disquiet; they sensed her endurance, her concern to do well, tragic and boundless. They told her what they liked: light pasta, fish and local wines. With an imperceptible slide of the hips and a rustle of coarse fabrics she leaned towards them. A last ray of sunlight skimmed the floor, just short of the fireplace, a slender, peaceful shaft of pale light, a sweetness, peace at sunset, acquiescence in the coming night, in solitude; in the setting sun just above her temple they saw the white of her coif. When the time came to serve them she returned and whispered Messer; leaning his fist on his leg he rose to his feet and, followed by his pupils, approached the table.

They looked at each other, sometimes turned their eyes to see better. The pupils were very handsome; the eldest talked to the master, vividly and with broad movements, his eyes gleamed in the twilight. She watched the pupils, the old man with his pale eyes, served them without a word. Moved towards them lowering her eyelids.

When they talked to her, about the town and the country or the soup she served them, she replied with a rapid phrase in a low voice, then blushed, temples and brow, eyes glued to her work as to something that would protect her, the horizon she mustn't lose sight of, they observed her gleaming eyes and her lowered lids, the vein palpitating just under the skin, just above the collar of her dress, imagined her faded breast beneath the fustian. She was ageless. Dogs barked; she gave a faint start, looked out of the window.

The sun disappeared behind the limes of the avenue. For a moment it skimmed the edge of the table, and the apron drawn up over her hip, her pale arm.

They put off climbing the stairs to the bedrooms, and often well after night had fallen they lingered near the fires or went out on to the terraces when, with mildness and pale clouds, they felt the fine days coming. They talked about the country and the people here, about the light over the river. They asked her questions about the river and the banks of the river, and the forest that began beyond the slopes, the roads that led through it to the peat bogs, slowly, choosing their words; sometimes it was as though they were singing. They planned journeys, said they were going to travel the country from north to south and from the east to the other river, to go to Romorantin where the castle had to be rebuilt and from there to Bourges via the forest and the lowlands. They would have to drain the land between the rivers and channel the turbid water into the ditches, irrigate the lands for corn, bring the Loire as far as Chambord and build a palace there, a hunting lodge for the king and the two queens. It wasn't for portraits or frescoes in their chapels they had brought him, he who wished for nothing now, who asked nothing of anyone and had worn out his eyes studying until some evenings he could barely see; it was so that he would supervise them in the way they needed and tell them how to do their work, ensure the perfection of the colonnades and cupolas and statues even more beautiful than those in the gardens of Tuscany a thousand years ago. They asked him to supply what was asked of Italians alone: beauty and, even more than beauty, the certainty of beauty. In return for the residence and the park and the river far below, in return for their admiration and their boundless goodwill – and all the honour was theirs, they said to themselves – he would devise palaces and staircases, he would study the façades and the depths of the gardens, the ditches, the mills, four at the entrance, four at the outlet, the profile of the rivers, the channels between them, and how to use sluice-gates to raise the water level and then eliminate the currents; he would plan dykes across the water, and ensure that the water left its sediment where it fell. He would leave with the pupils, travel the country as he had travelled Emilia and Romagna, Umbria and the Tiber valley, drawing, calculating, compiling maps and charts, painting if there was time left over. They served, they had always served, each in his own way, even the oldest of them; at the age of twelve in the *botteghe* they tempered the plaster, pounded the earth, the amber and powders, with rolled-up sleeves, gaily coloured in robes that beat against their calves they came and went between the lime, the gold and the stucco, the silver of the Alps. Together like the chants they heard at evening from the Signoria they depicted the angel of the Annunciation, cast the bells of Pistoia or sculpted David's hair in bronze; at evening they left for the town to deliver portraits and crests for helmets. The sons of peasants, of butchers and tanners, soon to be masters of perspective and fresco-painting, who made in silence what the masters, the real ones, ordered for their palaces, their wild dreams, forbidding them to make anything of their own invention, decreeing and deciding every detail: on this side the Virgin in a crimson dress lined with green gold, over there the saints and the angels, and behind them the roofs and the colonnades of the town, the façades and the porti-coes reproduced with great precision. They painted beautiful faces and loose hair, great battles and the gleaming bodies of magnificent horses, and that story of the man-god in which all desire and pun-ishment always started over again; they did their work, they supplied glory and beauty, sometimes without even noticing. With a line, a gesture, they kindled the dream, those worlds beyond where man reigned in such beauty beneath the chapel arches, naked, as disturbing as the God who with his finger gave him life. When they died they were spoken of, the master Giotto and the master Masaccio and the master Alberti, and the master della Francesca. When they had finished they decorated the masters' rooms and organized their feasts and funerals (what they had to say they did not say, waiting and then waiting some more, the years and death caught up with them, they would not say it, would never say it, that was how things were), draped with black the bedrooms of the palaces, organized the mourning, surrounded the female dead with satins and silks and all the gold in creation, so much so that the ambassadors marvelled, really what they saw in Italy surpassed in splendour anyone's imagination (for days and days knights and horses criss-crossed the town, followed with candles and torches by the raga-muffins of the outskirts, in other streets or the same as the ones in the plague years, they – their sons or their fathers – piled up by the doors of the houses in the crippling summer heat, until decomposed well beyond carrion, the carts came to collect them by the spadeful). Sometimes leaving feasts and chapels, men and gods with their unsettling bodies, or virgins in velvet and crimson taffetas, they went in search of other masters, in other countries and other towns where everything would start over again. Everything always started over with things foretold. Death alone would put an end to it.

There were evenings when they said nothing, others when they talked loudly, something in their voices that spoke of astonishment or confusion, then long silences, or else the eldest of the pupils would address the master, his voice hoarse and singing, he would rise to his feet and walk around him; in silence the master listened and while they spoke he looked at her, watched her, and she in turn faced them. Her eye, he observed, was furtive and hungry for knowledge, a moment later darting away; at other times she went on not seeing them, sitting on her stool she rubbed her barley bread with garlic and chives, ate in silence, bolt upright and knees tight together beneath the broad folds; in the hollow of the material they saw the blue shadow, and in the middle of the shadow the chunk of bread; later with a rustle of skirts she came over and held out an apple from the fire or a glass of *clairet* wine. Sometimes she left them in the kitchen, and took the air on the bench by the boxwood bushes. The wind dropped and the sky above the river grew thick, heavy and grey, the sound of the horses reached them, there were four of them in the stable and two ageing mares, the bay mare and the grey; they were to set off for the forest castles to get more. They went on talking.

He looked at the country and the colours of the sky over the river; one last time he sought grandeur and beauty, imagining on the white cliffs villas like the ones in Tuscany, the endless depth of the terraces. Withdrawing for days at a time to the studio where he asked them not to disturb him he designed a staircase, the highest and the broadest ever seen, which everyone would be able to go up and down without noticing anyone else doing the same. Sometimes his arm, his fingers, ceased to obey, they clenched paralyzed on the pencils. At other times his hand shook, gave way. He explained to the pupils, they drew what he told them. In the evening as they slept he looked at the drawings, made corrections, rethought. In ink, in lead pencil, black stone, thickening lines, adjusting calculations. In the margins he would add a commentary, an idea.

Italians came, made a carving of the castle in wood, designed the arcades, the staircases and the roofs over the terraces. In Milan he had redesigned the castle, with bridges, domes and cupolas, three long rows of arcades one above the other, majestic staircases and roofs over the terraces, deep, encrusted with white and green tiles, antique marbles, gardens of orange and citrus trees. The king approved and talked about the Charterhouse in Pavia or Poggio Reale near Naples. The work would start before the year was over, architects, masons and stonecutters were called to the peat bogs. The dream, the river and the canals, white stone palaces, would soon gleam beneath the sun, feasts and masquerades, processions of boats, brass sounding high and loud with pomp and splendour, the sovereigns would receive their glories and delights from God, two hundred and fifteen bedrooms made for love, not one less. He noted that the water could be dammed above the town, it would be possible to guide the river from Villefranche, and this task could be performed by the local people. The beams of the houses would be carried by boat to Romorantin and the river dyked high enough that it could be brought down along a gentle slope several leagues to the town.

*T*he sun rose in the sky, touching the summits of the great yews, soon bathing the courtyard in light. Crouched on her heels she washed the pots with sand she took from a basin; he came out, went round to the back of the house and asked them to prepare the horse, then walked down to the stables.

He set off on the jennet via the cliff road, through the acacia woods at the top of the town. He was going to see the king, to tell him his thoughts about the glorious dream and the castles to be built, the river to be diverted from its course. On some days when the sky was bright the table was set by the windows and they looked at the island planted with poplars and all around the river so wide one would have thought it was two rivers running side by side; the island was called the Island of Gold because of the light on the water morning and evening. Or else he rode for an hour or two towards Montlouis and Chaumont, looked at the river, the pale, iridescent light, the water on some days almost motionless, as though it had been halted, caught in a greyness that gleamed with light and fathomless gold. A child ran along the road singing, one foot to the other, sang, passionately, the moment all that mattered, joys glimpsed all at once, mad and intense as the joys of love.

Coming back, just before the town he dismounted, unhooked the bottle of ink attached to the saddle and sitting in the grass he drew, the island and the shores, further down towards the setting sun the place where the sky met the river, the pale horizon smoothed by mist, the grey gold in the river. Later when the feeling came he could not tell if it was what he saw or if it was death whose approach he felt now, at the same time each evening.

When he came back she was outside on a bench. She looked as though she was waiting, or else she had gone out for the spring evening and the warm wind. How could one tell? She barely turned her head when he arrived, she was mending a shirt or a little sheet, darning a sock; she looked at him then lowered her eyes as though already ignoring him. He crossed the terrace with a heavy, tottering tread, the vaguely erratic gait of someone who has spent all day on horseback. He came close to where she sat and greeted her in passing, talked to the pupil Melzi or the pupil Salai, to Battista, they led the horse to the drinking trough. Evening was falling on the terraces, the air smelled of boxwood. A moment later, before they had even seen her getting to her feet, she was by the fire taking the cauldron off the flames. The table had been set long before. She said she was ready.

All through spring and into the last days of June they heard the great hunts; further away in the forest they had hung cloths and they were running the roe deer, the king's archers, carts carrying the tents that the valets would erect in the clearings in the evening. The sound of the packs came to them on the wind, they heard the dogs, the animals at bay. She came outside and looked towards the shores, the tops of the valleys; she said that sometimes the animals fled all the way here, came through the vines, hoping to find thickets beside the river.

When they asked she told them news of the town, talked about the people who had made a bad name for themselves, the ones the gallows in front of the church had been built for, well-poisoners, child-killers. Over by St Denis a mule-thief had been pulled behind a cart, and finally whipped in front of the church. She did not raise her voice, talked of joy and sadness in the same quiet way. Sometimes she grew breathless as she talked, a lovesick lady from Montlouis had sunk laden with taffetas and gold necklaces to the bottom of the river.

*H*e set off for the forest with the pupil Salai and the pupil Melzi, the pupil Fanfoia, travelled with them through the moors and the peat bogs, studied the course of the rivers; the pupil Melzi spoke French, explained maps and books and what the peasants at the side of the road were saying. It took them eleven days to cross the forest and eleven days to travel the plains and hills towards Bourges, Nevers and Mâcon; the weather was fine, they rode in the woods and thickets, stopped beside ponds; on the way back they lingered in the village squares, looking at the Virgins and the stories of the saints in the churches. When they came back they drew castles, the channels that would link the Saône to the Loire, the region between the rivers, town by town, hill by hill. They talked about peat bogs and swamps, told the story of their journey. She listened to them, the swamps she knew well, at five in the evening the blue smoke rising from the land and feet sinking into grass as they would in the sand by the river. She poked the fire beneath the cauldrons; night fell and down from the shores came the smells of burnt grass, of freshly turned earth. From the farms they heard dogs barking. When they sat by the windows on the heights she saw the fires of the hovels, or further away the torches of the castle guards. She looked at her hands in the hollow of her skirts, rubbed them gently as though to banish a pain.

He took the pen and trimmed it, tried it out on a corner of the page; sitting on the terrace he wrote in notebooks, drew, annotated drawings, went on doing what he had always done, he had always written in notebooks; in the evening he lined them up in a cupboard in his room, twenty-five small books and two bigger books and sixteen even bigger than that, six books bound in vellum, another covered with green chamois leather; he wrote, made records and lists, water, fires, wars and floods, animals, things visible and invisible, everything that there was to know of the earth and the sky; he copied out the books lest he forget them, sitting on the terrace with a notebook on his knees he wrote, sometimes he stopped and looked around him, asking someone to go and get him another notebook; he passed his hand over his eyes; weary, he stretched his legs in the sun. He had always studied, he had come here with the books still to be read, he would read them before he died, copy out more pages. Ideas came, he drew an arch for Montlouis, and behind the arch a long avenue. He noted the dimension of the stones, the breadth of the arch. He saw her walking across the terrace with her buckets and stumbling over the gravel, when she passed in front of the stable the horses whinnied, she said something he didn't catch and went on her way; sometimes she limped on the sand in the avenues, he saw her limping, went on writing; gently the wind came, a wind from the river, he saw the oaks moving and on the terrace the tops of the great yews. With a gust of wind her skirts flew up, making her laugh or grumble; he wondered what she was thinking about, and how she managed sometimes and how she would take the coming weather. In between his scientific entries he jotted down the expenses for the studio and the house, clothes, fabric for hose 4 pounds 5 sols, lining 16 sols, tailoring 8 sous, Salai 8 sous, jasper ring, crazed stone, 13 sols, 11 sols. Noted the objects to be taken on journeys, into exile. Lists from the very beginning from his time in Florence and his time in Milan.

Knives with sharpened blades and smaller knives for trimming pens, beret and slippers, leather waistcoat, blue spectacles, his eyes were tired already, dye for the clothes, sheets of Spanish leather, white paper books, ink and crayons, palette, sponge, canvas, thread, needle. Bow and cord, market books. Large and small bowls, cups, chandeliers, four lengths of sheet, table-cloth, hand towel, shirts, small blankets. Two boxes to be put on the freight-saddle. Grammar of Lorenzo de' Medici, mappa mundi of Giovanni Benci, form for letters, lives of the philosophers. Aesop. The Lapidarium. Dante. Archimedes. Psalms. *On the Floods of the Nile* by Aristotle. To check that cloth boiled in vinegar is waterproof. Have three books bound. Find a boy to act as model. In the margin, angels, flowers, porphyry and chalcedony, beautiful hair, faces noticed in the street and in hospices. Tragic, nameless. Naked old men at death's door. Bohemians. Old women's breasts. Smiles of Madonnas ascending to heaven. On the day of Mary Magdalene in 1490 Giacomo came to live with me. For the expense he gives a florin, some bread, some wine, eggs, clay. Oil. For barber and buskins. Three sols left. Giacomo Salai. Eats for four, breaks flagons and spills wine on the table-cloths in the houses. Lies. Steals Turkish leather from the duke's stablemen to make himself a pair of boots or to buy some aniseed sweets. To calm him down he gives him a bow, a ring and ribbons and for his fifteenth birthday a whole piece of silver brocade. Clearly, making notes calms him down, brings order to his soul, to life. Drives away the shadows. On the ninth day of July 1504, Wednesday, at seven o'clock Ser Piero, my father, died. Sometimes nothing, just a date. This St Mary's Day, mid-August in Césène. Re-reading it he would know what it meant. Too great a joy or sadness, things that cannot be said (and had to see it written down to say it to himself and then to believe it, and the maddest moments, were they enough to consign the rest to oblivion, the days before and the days after so grey they made you want to die?); he flicks, deciphers, seeks, no longer really knows, at other times in a flash he remembers. Those moments, joy, sadness, he could count them on the fingers of both hands, maybe even one. When he leaves a notebook in his bedroom or his studio, he asks her to go and get it. She rises to her feet and hurries, brings it back at arm's length like the priest at the offertory handing the host to the faithful. In the corner of a page he adds an angel, curly hair, pale eyes.

H^e watched her finishing her soup on her corner of the table, said to himself she had always eaten her soup in silence on a corner of the table. That she was thinking of the peat bogs. Remembering a table-cloth bordered with blue stripes. Remembering a grey wall hung with bowls and curry combs. A horsehair bed by the fire and the woodworker with the little axe who had made it. One of those narrow, dark hovels where, morning and evening, the chimneys spewed out their smoke and water rose from the ground, streamed cold and grey over the walls. He imagined her sitting on a bench in the evening sun, sorting apples, unwinding skeins, the farmyard smelled of horses and milk from the byre, the heather exhaled its unsettling, dry fragrance, the last sounds came from the village, then the neighbours arrived, took up their places around the fire, told stories, the things of life, tragic and nameless. In the middle of the stories they heard the black beast, hoarse cries from the depths of the forest, the dogs barking. Still later in the thick silence, in the thick and heavy solitude of the forests, the fathers came home; in the shadows of the sheets they covered the mothers, rooted and rummaged in them for a good long while then with a great noise, a rasping sound coming from who knows where, they would crash down on them and go to sleep. With a blow of their hips the women would send the men rolling to the other end of the palliasse and, as they did every evening, burst into tears.

She got up and looked towards the terraces, went over to the fire; with one hand she lifted a lid, with the other she poured in the white wine and the verjuice and plunged in the spoon, studied the broth, climbed on to a stool and lit the chimney candles; on a table she put the bowls, the jug of wine, the water, the bread.

The brothers and sisters died of bad milk, bad heat or the damp rising from the earth. The fathers and mothers wept or didn't weep, from one year to the next they grew resigned, branded the animals, rebuilt ditches or rid the fields of stones, scythed the oats, the wheat, the rye and bound them into sheaves, brought in the harvests. When they had finished they set the wine flowing and walked in the streets to honour God and give alms-bread to those poorer than themselves, from blossoming Easter to Maundy Thursday they walked amid prayers and penitence, and in September they exalted the Holy Cross, asking forgiveness from St John, that he might cast the demon from the herds, they made the animals walk over coals.

One day she had left the bogs, the deep forest. Like others she had walked to the river where the masters dwelt in white stone houses, she had walked ten days with the baby to the town by the river. It had been summer; she washed in the rivers and the donkey grazed on the embankment. She had arrived where the masters lived, like the others who had come from the forest she had swept the floors and spread out the heather in great armfuls, scoured the bowls, washed and mended the linen and the blankets, grown used to the masters, watched them being born and dying, making love and weeping by night in the bed-rooms, rising in the morning and striding away, hips swinging, to war or off on their travels, coming back with marble statues and Venice crystals, basins for their gardens, celebrating their return with the gold and silk of the masquerades. When, one day after all that love and war, drunkenness or despair, succumbing to catarrhs and jaundice they went to bed, these women were there behind the alcove drapes sponging brows, hearing last words. Later on they washed them, pale rough linen they took from the wardrobes, unfolding it then rolling it around the corpses, skins with a sad and sweetish smell, the smell of those whose life was ebbing, men, women, children, the work was the same, the women barely looked at them; when their work was done they followed them to the grave, in the freshly turned earth they planted candles and torches while the poor prayed, as numerous and as fervent as alms permitted. Soon they sought masters in other houses where all of life and death was starting over again, everything was always starting over.

She finished setting the table, he saw her back and the loose hair emerging from under her coif, her plait, her weary shoulders. Sometimes without their asking her anything she spoke. Slowly, in a low voice. In a big patch of blue sky washed with white and rain, a great commotion of horses and coaches on the cobbles of Bout-des-Ponts, she had seen the king's people returning, three thousand on foot and on horseback, litters and carts carrying beds and curtains, chests filled with scarlet and grey satin, linen shirts from Coutances, fine embroidered fabrics from Venice, blue diamonds;

they had all gone in search of money in the *bonnes villes* of the lowlands, had travelled the provinces as far as the sea, and to the east as far as the rim of the mountains, crossed the villages on their beautiful horses, breathed in the slurry of summer farmyards, the scent of nurses sitting unbuttoned outside the houses. In turn they talked about it as they would have talked about a fresco they had painted on a wall, men and horses in procession, and down below, when they were coming back, the river, the sun lighting the shores. Further behind, bringing up the rear of the procession, the servants and courtesans seated on mules.

When she had finished she sat down for a moment by the window and looked outside or else looked at her hands, crossing and uncrossing them in the hollow of her skirts. Silence fell. They turned towards her, asked a question or said a few words, an idea, something that needed doing over the next few days; she looked at them, looked at the master, with a nod of her head she showed that she had understood, if an answer was needed she gave an abrupt yes or no and without further comment, then she turned towards the cliffs.

She got used to it, that's what they finally said to themselves; she talked to the people from the farm when they delivered bushels of beans and cart-loads of wood, she said there would be a frost that night, they would have to keep the straw on the summer flowers. In the castle they were making preparations for weddings and a baptism, they were raising the terraces on the outskirts of town up as far as Notre Dame, and in the middle of the field they were going to have a battle, six hundred men on one side and six hundred on the other, with lances and armour, that's what they were saying in town. It started raining, the light soft-ened into ochres and grey, the steam rose gently from the slopes. Or else she talked about the wind that had risen, she had seen the *gabarres*, the flat-bottomed cargo-boats, coming back up the river, the full square sails bringing the boats towards Orléans on the river swell; for more than ten days they had been waiting for the wind and now there was a gale blowing, in the park with Battista she had collected broken branches, she had made a pile of them in the woodshed. Several times on Sunday she left, she said she had things to attend to over by Artigny, they saw her going off with the donkey, when she came back night was falling; she served them as she did on the other days and without a word as soon as the table was cleared she went to her garret.

He looked at her as one looks at something one is discovering, without favour or indulgence. During the last days of spring she had to get used to his gaze upon her, telling herself that the master was able to observe the servant as he might observe a tree or a colour in the sky, a corpse in a grave. Sometimes the most unexpected things could quietly, peacefully become so banal and ordinary that life was even harder in their absence; when he turned away she noticed, then with apparent indifference turned away as well. He talked about habits, about things beginning and things coming to an end.

He drew a face, neither a man nor a woman nor a child, looked in boxes of old drawings, the pale eye beneath the transparent lid, the mass of curls, started over again, made comparisons. In Italy they had talked about the angel, about the delicacy of the bruised and budding flower, the hollow of the shadow on the cheek, that sense of heat, of burning skin, emotion, pleasure; how could one tell, sometimes everything had been so magnificent.

*W*hen the fine weather came she swapped her fustian skirts for skirts of finely striped fabric, grey and brown beneath the blue apron, and in the evening after dinner she made herself a petticoat and a bodice from cotton bought from the mountain pedlar, the one who sat outside St Martin's selling pins and ribbons, embroidered shawls and Our Lady of Mercy in his big coat.

They stayed late on the terraces and talked until nightfall as they had done in the gardens of the Signoria when they were drawing ancient marbles, still talking about shadow and light and the brilliant colours of the northern masters; they talked about the departure of the pupil Salai, he was going back to Italy, that was what they said in the evening on the terraces; they raised their voices, she looked at them, trying to understand, probably understanding. Sometimes they had bad news to relate, the travellers who had come from Italy reported that some important frescoes were being damaged, were breaking down in the bitter clamminess of the churches, the ones they had taken months and years to paint hoisted on scaffolding in the cold gloom of the chapels; they talked about the other ones, never begun or left unfinished, abandoned when doubts arose and nothing more could be done. Messer the painter lost his reason, to paint horses he locked himself in the libraries of Florence and read every book ever written on horses, he never stopped, would never stop, he was mad and something else was troubling him; for the Adoration he designed enormous staircases coming from nowhere and going nowhere, men and horses mad with misery and breasts offering themselves up to wounds, despair, tumult, applied shade to shade, deferring the colour and the moment of completion. In carts from the *podere* the monks delivered bundles of firewood, oil and sheaves of wheat, on the first of the month they brought him the money he needed for his colours. He did not add the colours, would never add them. He left them the staircases, the wingless, colourless angels and the mad horses and set off for Milan to find another master. A hundred leagues and twelve days of travel towards the northern mist, the cold of the Lombardy plains.

One December evening he arrived at the foot of the ramparts and crossed the parade ground. Amid the servants and horses afflicted by the same strange fever, he made lists of unknown words to calm himself down; although he was not even aware of it he was waiting for someone to arrive, someone he didn't even know existed. Page after page he copied out the books so as not to forget them, drew in the margins or worked with a silver nib on grey paper, blue paper. Learned Latin, ceaselessly conjugating the verb to love. Had no idea what was to come.

Through the window he saw her moving away towards the end of the park. She went down to wash the linen in the river, not waiting until the baskets were full. As though for the pleasure of it. The wind lifted her skirts. She walked with a courage that made one think of happiness. Behind her the donkey came forward with the panniers, peaceful, sometimes joyful – a bray or a prank, a short sideways gallop. The sun rose in the sky, haloed the fog above the foliage, just before the river. The shadows were deep against it.

When she came back up the avenue she was smiling. Her small pale outline gleamed in the morning. He was grateful to her for that. He thought she knew nothing of crazed imaginings, dreams of joy or pleasure. He thought she had known neither worry nor expectation. Nor the fear of losing everything. That she had kept herself apart, out of prudence, happy with the calm days, the bowl of soup and the fresh bread in her cloth in the morning on the corner of the table, and in the evening the smell that rose from the earth, the steps of the horses returning.

Peaceful she was those days, more serene than anyone. She went to hang the linen in the garden then returned to fetch it in, folded it into the baskets; she lingered by the back gate, picked herbs for soup. Later she asked them to help her fold the sheets, when she saw the clouds gathering on the horizon, light, transparent, she said it would be fine again tomorrow. He thought of the old woman who had waited for him for twenty years in the hills near Empoli.

The pupils had set off for Romorantin, there were measurements to be taken, sketches to be made of the town and the ramparts; he had not gone with them, had said it was because of the wind, had stayed with her and the Italian man-servant. Summer was coming, the sun rose early, a blue light on the trees in the park; he rested. In the morning she set off at the same time, put on her cape over her grey dress and went down to look for the donkey and the panniers; she took the low road, passed along the outskirts to the Rue des Bouchers. He watched her setting off on the donkey. In his notebook he wrote out his expenses, bread and flour, fish, cheese, wildfowl. The rest, oil, shanks of beef and pork for pickling in brine, arrived from the farms along the shore or else they went to fetch them. The sun rose in the sky; he saw the blue mist spreading around the roofs. There were mornings when the light was blue, it rose from the river, and there was no way of telling where the sky began and the river stopped. In the distance from the bedroom windows he saw the river moving towards the sea, a great broad river running between the shores of pale sand. He wrote letters, talking of life here and the work on the castle, what the pupils were doing. He said he could no longer tell how long he had been away, that everything confused him at times and that he hadn't forgotten anyone down there, he asked for news of Milan and Florence and what was happening in Rome, he said he would not be coming back, that the pupil Salai was going back to the country, he had been working with him for more than twenty years now. He had not forgotten the summers, the evening conversations in the gardens, among the marble statues and the lions of the Signoria crouching behind the grilles, breathing the fragrance of the jasmine and the white rose-bushes, talking so long that sometimes they saw the sun rising over the hills. Sometimes he would write in a notebook: today Giacomo Salai set off for Italy again. As he had always done. He would write. He would remember. He forgot. Said he forgot. Let the time pass, as he had done when he had been ill, fevers caught in the swamps, for whole days on horseback he had breathed the heat and miasma of Romagna, trying to work out how to drain it of its putrid waters and guide them to the sea; he suffered from fevers and his eyes could no longer see, he had worn them out reading day and night; he remembered nights in the Belvedere in the Pope's apartments, he remembered his frailty, the sweetness of frailty and how he was able to glimpse the end of things without pain. He put down the notebooks and closed his eyes. Listened to the sounds of summer, looked at the wind on his skin. The castle would be built or would not be built, in Romorantin or elsewhere – in the end what did it matter, what would remain of him but the three paintings he had brought here on the backs of mules, in the inns evening after evening putting them at the head of his bed wrapped with the sheets and blankets which protected them and which sometimes he removed with one hand before going to sleep, revealing the canvas and observing it by candlelight, faces wrought from shadow, transparent flesh, the three paintings commissioned by no one, and which would never leave him.

When the pupils returned they talked of their journey, showed plans and sketches, the work they had done down there; he would study the sketches with them, draw a façade, pediments, a terraced roof, beyond the gates avenues of yews and white stone arches; disappearing into the distance they would see the flower-beds and lawns and the rare species they had brought from Tuscany and Emilia. Then the pupil Salai would leave for the lowlands and the mountains, retread the whole road back to Italy, to the vines of the Porta Vercellina that he was giving him. He would build his house in the vines; he said he would never forget the master and that he would write every week, he would give his letters to the man who crossed the mountains from Milan, and who in Lyons passed the mail on to others who would bring it here at a gallop, two weeks not more and they would have his letters, that's what he said. He would tell them about Italy, about their friends and relations who had stayed down there. About the frescoes on the walls of the churches and the great horses fading in the bitterness of the saltpetre. About the angel of the Baptism, the first work. He thought of the angel. Of the face drawn a thousand times. Of summer down there and the great heat, of the shadow of the trees on the roads, on the roads in shafts of light the brilliant shadow of the foliage. He would let the pupil Salai go back on his own, he would stay, it was here that he would die.

He waited for her to come back. It was barely nine o'clock. He heard the donkey on the cobbles and her voice shouting, when he leaned forward into the gallery he saw her, red-faced, dishevelled, pulling the donkey who refused to move. Sometimes she lingered in the part of town called Bout-des-Ponts where the fishermen were, watching the flat-bottomed boats and the rafts sailing down the river, bringing up to Nantes faiences from Nevers and wines from Beaune, heavy wooden boards. On those days she came back a little later. From the porch he saw her hurrying, unloading the panniers and going without a word to the cupboards and the chimney where she tended to the fire.

At some point or another he came to find her, it was a kind of appointment with her. He took up his position by the windows or if it was cold by the chimney at the table itself where without speaking or even looking at him she prepared the meal. She turned towards the terraces, the sun that whitened the sand of the avenues then all of a sudden disappeared behind a cloud; she set off for the cellar to draw the wine, fetch oil and verjuice; in the hollow of her skirts she peeled vegetables. She talked about the drawings, said she looked at them sometimes, they were very nice drawings. Talked about the pupil Salai and his leaving. Talked about the angel. First encountered in an alleyway in the Armoreri district, swords, cuirasses and bucklers. Dirty, verminous. Insolence on his lips. They said the women and children of Nubia, beyond the Nile, had the same expression. He looked at the child and didn't touch him, except to wash him because he was always dirty, drew him, a transparent expression beneath heavy lids, opening his eyes, closing them, smiling, sleeping. And soon, naked on horseback. Now a child of the gods he mounted bareback and galloped into the Lombardy plain as though barbarian hordes were hot on his heels. He remembered. Forgot. It was the year when the Genovese, reworking Ptolemy's calculations and re-reading Marco Polo, came within a hundred leagues of Thule – the sea he said on his return was not yet frozen – set off for Madeira in the Azores and finally visited the coasts of Guinea, went in search of the silk road via the coast of Africa. He had not yet crossed the Great Sea, knew nothing of the islands where the east winds would take him, knew nothing of worlds yet to be discovered. They spoke of the sea and the great voyages, the ones who had seen

Prester John and the great Khan in Babylon, and the men who threw the bodies of the dead to the birds, who drank blood, who offered their wives to strangers. In the boats on their return they brought back balm and diamonds, gold and silks, brown-skinned women. In Ragusa men who were neither Christian nor Saracen lived like animals and sold themselves for nothing in the city markets.

She watched him drawing, he drew the angel – the angel closed his eyes, opened them, turned away – the skies in the storm, faces, faces. Finally they talked of the sea.

(She imagined the sea, and water wherever you looked, water as far as the boundless horizon, the great waves and the ceaseless sound like the sound of the river on the stones in the middle of the bed, the crash of the water against the stones, day and night, the sound she liked; she imagined the ones who crossed the sea, who went all the way to strange countries where the sun burned, and sometimes the rain fell stormily, they left every-thing, knew they wouldn't return, they must have lost hope; sometimes she talked, a quick word uttered and her eye turned away, like a question she had asked, the phrase lingered in the air; she rose to her feet and added logs of holm oak to the fire, a good wood she used to say, it burned nice and slowly under the pots; she adjusted the andirons, poked the fire beneath the spits, talked about the sea and the river and the cloudy sky, the colour of the river, the lighter water towards the middle of the bed; she had seen the queen in her *galiot* heading for the sea, she had seen the great yellow sails the men had hoisted just off the island, in the bend in the wind-swollen river the tartans turned golden by the sun; she talked of the sea, of the ones who left, who went in search of the world, the four rivers of paradise. She understood.)

Sometimes her movements grew slower – weariness or a moment's hesitation, or the time it took her to do things – so slow they tended towards stillness, barely discernible like glances between closing lids, nothing moved now but the fire in the chimney, the wood slowly sweating its final sap and all of a sudden spraying sparks towards the top of the fireplace. As though time was stopping, as though the time needed to take heart had ceased to move, time stood still, simply and so intensely that perhaps there was nothing else to be hoped for. He could make out her expression beneath her unmoving, transparent eyelid, fixed like the delicately wrought clay of porcelain figures. He looked at her as he would have looked at a stranger, turned towards her, looked after her when she moved away without a word.

Summer settled in. Day after day they admired the light, the quiet, gleaming blue. On the roads the women returned carrying sheaves over their shoulders, they walked beside the mules and the great armfuls of grass beating their flanks, struggled as they approached the slope. She talked about the summer and the yellowing corn. About the light on the river. He talked about the light, and how the shadows weren't the same, about Tuscany and its great heat, childhood summers. He recalled the gleaming shade beneath the foliage, horse rides in the hills and the mountains when he returned to the country, deep valleys and steep paths; from far off he saw the dog roses and the rows of vines, the pink roofs surrounding the steeple. His mother was waiting, she had made lunch and put out the table-cloth, as lovely as the June evening when she had been tumbled in a hay-barn, Ser Piero a young lawyer and the descendant of lawyers was a great lover of women, so much so that as he held a woman close he didn't know if what he had in mind was a future wedding or a pleasure to come, violent and oblivious to everything else; alone in the hillside farm the peasant woman had given birth, discreet and furtive, as calmly terrified as a spawning bitch; he watched her in her blue dress, the great blue light that on summer evenings allowed a glimpse of brown flesh, and all the time he watched her he remembered the past, behind the glances, the smells, he sought the warmth and fragrance of her skin, pictures, pictures, a smile one day, how would you put it, while already, he remembered that too, he was imagining his old age and her death; she would die, there were days when he imagined only that and the time passing, passing endlessly; he guessed he must have seen her about twenty times after leaving Tuscany, twenty times she must have watched him come back along the path through the vines and opened her arms to him, twenty times since Venice, Rome and Milan he had come to inhale the smell of her skin and of her clothes; the smell changed from year to year, who could tell after all, changed until one day it became that smell of weariness, the sour, sad scent of little old women worn out by life who no longer had anything to lose or fear, not death or even unbearable abandonment.

He said he loved the summer, he would have liked to enlarge the park, draw arches at the end of the terraces, plant trees there that he would have liked to see growing bigger, cypress trees like the ones over there on the hills, great poplars and other green oaks. He drew the avenues towards the river and he saw her coming up the avenues with her skirts in the wind, then he gave up the park, gave up tomorrows, drew heads of curly hair, cats, peacefully open hands, thought of the death to come, what the last years would be like. The pupil Salai had left, he had gone with him as far as Gué-Péan before the forest; one morning at dawn she had seen them crossing the terraces with their horses, passing the arch and moving away via the cliff road, they had dismounted by the entrance to the pines, before the hamlets that gleamed some way off in the midday sun. They had looked at one another one last time, later, he himself could not have said for how long, he had seen him moving off on his horse, the horse as black as himself on which he had come from Italy; he had stayed motionless on his mount waiting for him to disappear, to become an imperceptible dot towards the slopes where sometimes even now among the foliage he spotted him, then he could see him no longer.

When he sat by the windows he saw the cliffs and the castle walls, behind them he could make out the river and the sun on the pale sand. He thought of all the lands they had crossed to come here, he thought about the things he would not see again, everything shrank, and taste, love, passed away. The sharpness of things. He said to himself that he was not unhappy. Her work finished and the table laid she would sit down, at some point or other she would take her seat opposite him by the windows or the chimney, she waited for the chickens to finish roasting, or waited until they themselves were ready for supper. The fire made her eyes shine, coloured her face, the fair skin fading around her eyelids. She looked at his hands or over by the window the trimmed boxwood bushes, gently brushed by the sun. Bitter and warm, peaceful, their scent entered the kitchen. She was there and not there, he didn't know what she was thinking about.

*W*hen they went to the farms they took her along with them. They went to fetch oil or the quarters of beef and pork that she would salt, they took the road that ran along the river and further along, after the villages, met up with the forest again. The summer was hot, without wind or the slightest breeze from the slopes, the road stretched out between rye and wheat, ran along the motionless river; after the copses it reached the horizon, on all sides they saw the horizon and the sky white with heat. She knew that road, she had come that way when she had left the peat bogs. When she had come to serve in the houses along the river. It was summer like now, she said.

Over by Artigny after the last houses on the slope, they saw a woman. She was walking along the side of the path, coming and going under the trees or sometimes lying down further away in the ditch of a vine; when they passed they saw her pale flesh, abundant among the hoisted fabric, a smile on her lips. They watched her in silence. They arrived and loaded the jars and the hanks of meat on to the mules, they walked along by the ponds for a while and let the animals drink. The men talked about the fires in the copses further down towards Pont-Levoy, it was so hot that the earth they said had begun to burn, the ground had been consumed for a whole length of thicket, narrow smoke, quick and tenacious as though born of the earth itself, people from Theray and Grand-beauvais had come with carts and buckets, had put out the first fires. By the time they came back the sun had reached the opposite shore, turning the banks golden, the woman had gone or else she was still there with her skirts lifted, they passed without looking, she on her mount as straight as anything and her eyes set far ahead. Sometimes she disappeared behind a hedge, getting tangled up in the skirts that she crumpled with a faint crunch; when she came back to them she trotted on the donkey, lips closed and eyes fixed on the furthermost horizon. Later in the sun they noticed the whiteness of the walls of the little port, the pale shadows on the ground of the road. Four hours had passed in a few moments. As far as she could she looked for the cliffs and didn't take her eyes off them. They ran into muleteers returning from Montlouis and Chaumont, further down they saw a man crossing the river on his horse. When they reached the house they heard vespers ringing in the churches of St Denis and Notre Dame des Grèves.

Then she spoke. Red with fury, loud and clear so that they would hear. She talked about the woman on the slope and said that she would have her clothes torn off and be thrown naked to the dogs who would eat her, others had had to plead for mercy for less, bare-headed and a torch in her hand, to be pilloried three times on market days and beaten at the cross-roads. As for herself, for what she had to say about it, she would pray to God and the saints that the lice would devour her bones.

The heat grew more intense; she closed doors and shutters, taking shelter from the heat as a peasant-woman does, as one might take shelter from the enemy in a village besieged, she washed the house with great quantities of water, forever going to the well with her buckets, coming back and all of a sudden pouring them over the tiles; exhausted, she took off her coif as another woman might have pulled up her stocking, shedding her skin, revealing the invisible, the sun made her hair shine against the clear line. With one hand she smoothed the short hairs that grew in curls on her temple, still fair, half-way between fair and grey, then put her cloth coif back on, different according to whether one looked at her in shade or light, impossible to tell some days. Shortly after midnight she went down to the river. When she came back the bottom of her skirt was wet, like the curls escaping from the hairpin at the nape of her neck. He spent his day in the lower room studying machines or drawing; sometimes a letter arrived from Milan, another from Empoli, the pupil Salai or Lorenzo, one of his brothers giving news of the family; she brought them in without a word then, adjusting her coif or stuffing a corner of her apron back into her belt, vanished into the depths of the house. In the park the avenues hummed with bees, time stood still. When he woke from his siesta he saw her through the window crossing the terraces, then heard her footsteps on the gallery; later when the sun passed the poplars she went down to pick strawberries in the moss of the little wood, slowly coming back up the avenue with her basket. A little later still when he arrived in the kitchen she was eating on a bench against the cellar steps, studying him; he surprised her eye, which darted away, then the furtive and confused sound of skirts as, discovered, she stood up again. With apparent indifference she busied herself in a chest, stopped there and looked for a moment, finally taking out a dish towel, a table-cloth. He smelled the scent of roses from Provins that had been placed on the linen.

When on the river road they saw men going to Orléans to touch the chalice of St Euverte and the wood of the True Cross, she said summer was coming to an end.

*W*hen autumn arrived they barely noticed, the weather was so mild that they let the fires go out in the evening. Shortly before All Saints' the sky darkened. The warmth remained, a damp warmth that blew the smoke back down on the roofs, poisoned the gardens and terraces, the little wood towards the river with clamminess. Slowly, calmly the summer was ending. There was a sadness, the certainty that with summer something else was coming to a close.

She was the one who thought that, who conveyed it without words. Was it the heavy, grey sky, so heavy and grey that they wondered how they would ever see the sun again, or time that sometimes seemed to stand still, the astonishing silence around them, or something else they didn't know? During those days she showed a new restraint, a new attentiveness. Her movements grew slower, she came forward on tiny steps, so cautiously that one might have thought she was afraid of bumping into the space around her, dreaming, anxious as one is when waiting and everything seems to have become possible. They watched her, studied her way of staying aloof, of being alert like an animal that senses danger, without moving or making a sound, holding her breath.

The air smelled of the fires burning in the fallow land, the scents that rose from the slopes. The sky darkened again, warm, windless mornings and evenings. For days they surveyed the low, wet skies, opaque as sleep. They watched her as though she understood what was happening and would explain it to them; in the evening they came downstairs earlier and sat down around the fire, stretched their legs, brought their hands close to the flames. She inched forward in the candlelight, bent over, almost invisible in the narrow circle between table, boxes and fire where the shadows flickered. They barely spoke. Without having to say so they understood that she reigned in that kitchen as one might reign over an empire. In turn they fell silent, they waited.

He forgot the angel, abandoned the notebooks, he barely went out. He asked the pupils to take out the anatomical studies, he returned to the line of a muscle or a nerve, reddened a membrane or a tear, he explained it to the pupils, said that in order to paint a man's body they had to know what lay beneath the skin: bone, muscles and nerves, they had to know the invisible.

Travellers came to visit him; while the servants took their horses to be watered they lingered in the avenues and on the terraces, they walked out on the gallery from which they admired the park, came into the kitchen where she was hastily finishing the meal. Later when she served poultry and stews they said they had eaten nothing as good in Germany or Flanders or anywhere else they had been. They discussed the business of their countries, such long wars, the trees of the Rhine valley and Mont St Michel, from whose summit they said you could see as far as the edge of Spain. The pupils went to get their drawings. He explained how he had studied corpses in the hospices in Rome and Milan. The travellers were astonished, admired the beauty of the drawings and the study that had gone into them, asked if anyone had done anything like them before. He said he didn't know. When the travellers left she put the embers in the footwarmers and went upstairs to put oil in the lamps; they stayed in the kitchen talking, commenting on the day, breathing in the evening air. When her work was done she wished them goodnight and returned to her garret. From there she heard their voices and their laughter and the barn-owl hooting in the little wood by the river.

On St Martin's Day in November passing through the outskirts they saw the people coming for the fair; the streets were filled with smells, the stamping of hoofs. Sometimes they came from far away with nothing but the stuff in their baskets, their pins and ribbons, they stayed for the week and left for other fairs, other towns. It was said that the poor things roamed every kingdom, the world was nothing but a long strip of land beneath the sky, in the end if you walked long enough you came to a bottomless gulf; some people had wanted to go that far, wanted to point their feet only in that direction, had only ever wanted to do that, she knew some who had set off and never been seen again. They had said they were going to pray to St James or St Mary in far-off cathedrals, one day they had arrived, had cried *Sancte Jacobe! Sancte Jacobe!* and they had been buried on a hillside, a wooden cross planted at their heads. She said she had just seen two children who had only one body between them, they were in a little cart pulled by dogs, they were going to pray at Notre Dame de Cléry; their father, a shepherd, was walking near them, looking straight ahead, not taking his eyes off the horizon, she had seen them crossing the river towards Artigny.

Anticipating the winter he had boots made for her, and for her skirts he ordered an ell of fustian, 7 sols, to which he added, 4 sols, an ell of blue fabric for two Sunday bodices. He asked her if she had enough hats and hoods, she said she was fine as she was and he shouldn't worry about her.

He was drawing again, with fingers stiffened against his pencil he returned to his work for Santo Spirito and Santa Maria Novella, the bodies naked and exposed, opened up, and then drawn a whole winter long in the cellars at night, surveying the rooms amid the raucous sound of the voices and the sharp odour of the pallets. He had come to get them before they died, he wanted to know, to understand; sometimes they slept, he watched them sleeping behind the hemp curtains, already drawing death, the moments just before death in a violent, calm and despairing suspension of time. Later he opened them up along the middle, men, women, children (and sometimes in the bellies of the women the child who had died with them, curled up like a willing victim), he drew them, he remembered them talking, stretching out their hands, he thought of the dead old man sitting on the edge of the bed as they chatted, the mad-woman who had sung her old tunes by the river at night; she had lost her life so gently that everyone down there had dreamed of doing the same.

One evening before supper she had gone out to get some wood. He had seen her behind the sheds with her bundle of firewood, advancing on uncertain, tottering steps, neither her hip nor her leg follow-ing her stride; she limped through the terraces, she passed in front of him, then with a dry sound she broke the wood, one fistful after another she slid it under the logs. She had said nothing. Night was falling gently, soon she would collect the embers for the warming pans. When she turned to him he crossed the old pelisse over his chest and closed his eyes.

*S*he went on telling them news of the town, talking about the ones who had died after being kicked by a horse or catching cold in church; she talked about the river, the water that ran in circles and whirlpools, when they were mad they opened up and dragged in the unwary, beneath the seamen's arch they had found the body of a little shepherd from Chaumont whose mother had been calling for him for a whole year. She talked about the wolf hunts on the riverbanks over by Montlouis, and how after catching the dog-wolf in their canvases they went off ahead of the she-wolf in their boats and found her drowned. She said she had slept badly, the hen had been singing, the cock or the little owl had cried till morning. She spoke quietly, not raising her voice; when she spoke it was like a continuation of the silence. They heard the last carts leaving the outskirts, men playing cards and singing in the taverns. For their part they talked about Italy and the endless wars of the men still entering cities with their lances against their thighs, striking the walls high and low, conquering bastions and in the evening, loaded down with their booty and spoils, setting up camp in the valleys unaware who had just won the battle, they or the enemy; there was no end to the wars in Italy. They talked about great journeys and seas unknown, of the men who on their way westwards in search of gold and silk had one day put in at the great land of Orinoco: one evening they had reached the first of the islands, and without waiting any longer, thanking God on their knees, had in the presence of a notary taken possession of San Salvador of the Bahamas. Others were setting off there now, under burning suns they were opening up new territories, no longer thinking of anything but sugar cane and its mother-of-pearl stalks thrusting towards the pale sky, brown-skinned women, the warmth of the wind. A little later she went up to her garret, climbing the stairs with her crutch in her hand. Sometimes she missed a step. Without so much as a groan she climbed to the high, narrow cupboard, then nothing more was heard, not even the dry and crumpled sound of the palliasse when she went to bed. He imagined her sitting on the edge of the bed, unable to lie down, saying to herself that it was time to sleep, thinking of the closing day, of things done or said, making time last as long as she could, or, lying motionless watching the ceiling, all of a sudden slumping heavily into sleep, waking in the morning in the same position, her arms along her body wrapped in the rough night-shirt and her face exposed like the faces in churches of recumbent figures and verminous skeletons.

Sometimes she came towards him looking as though she was about to tell him something; he would run into her at the bottom of the staircase or on the terraces with her buckets or a bundle of firewood; he observed her hesitation, her almost imperceptible confusion, but a moment later with tiny movements she would adjust her hat, tap the front of her skirts to uncrumple them and flick away invisible carrot-tops. Continuing on her way she returned to the kitchen where someone was just arriving, then tightening over her dress the strings of her apron further away behind the tables she turned her back on them, noisily took the frying pans and the bowls out of the chests, and made pancakes or hot sweet milk. Later still he saw the grey of her eyes darkening, like a pond under a rainy sky. He came towards her and asked what was wrong. She said: Nothing, Messer, and moved away amid the exaggerated sound of her skirts.

*A*utumn passed, grey and warm; the first rains came in December with the west winds, from the horizon the clouds gathered over the town and all of a sudden burst on the rooftops, on the grey river where the waves ran. They thought of the winter to come, of the end of everything. They drew the storms, recalled the north wind and the earth when it shook, the volcanoes of Italy, Etna, Stromboli, the water, the wind and fire: if the earth was round then the water of the oceans and the rivers was suspended in the air, and every time the hurricanes rose whole countries could be swallowed up as it was said that whole cities had been swallowed by the sea. They went to see the flat-bottomed *gabarres* passing the bridge, dismasting at great speed and passing, one after the other, beneath the seamen's arch. They talked about the people whose bodies were crushed between the arch and the side of the *gabarres* or who fell into the river, who were hauled up on ropes. On still days men waited to return upstream, or tied themselves to the boats and with their feet in the water pulled along with the oxen, sometimes all the way from Nantes they returned to the high country on foot, stopped at the homes of people originally from here and asked for a place to sleep. Straw was laid out for them by the fireplace and the next day at dawn they set off on their way again.

They were coming into winter, coming into sadness. The time of courage. They were going to have to wait a while longer. For the signs of mildness, the blue in the sky and the sun that would warm the stones. In the evening she spent longer sitting by the windows, saying nothing and looking out, crossing and uncrossing her hands in the hollow of her skirts. He said to himself that every evening since she had started serving in the riverside houses she had sat by the windows, had crossed and uncrossed her hands in the hollow of her skirts, with things to say that she did not say and would never say, keeping them to herself and showing with bitter silences that she was keeping them to herself, as though keeping them to herself and showing that she was keeping them to herself were part of sadness and solitude, grey, interminable time, thinking of the misfortunes of time, of the hardness of life, of women lying in the vines. As for her, when they saw her lying down it would mean she was dead. Knowing nothing of abandon, of the very idea of abandon, gone with her sufferings and the things that should not be said, should not be confessed, to anyone, things to be kept to the end, praying to God that they did not come to her lips at the last moment. Yes, that was it, she thought about the things that were not to be said, to be kept to herself for ever.

*W*inter was hard that year. Shortly before Christmas the cold came and the rivers froze; further up behind the slope a cow calved in the snow. Birds fell on the roads, rigid in an instant, taken by the frost. They talked about the winter of 1510 in Florence when the rain froze in the sky, fell like diamonds into the streets (and the summer that had followed had been so hot that the plague and all the evils of hell had entered the city, three times the earth had trembled and the people had spent the night in the squares). They didn't go out much. They worked, designed machines; she saw them dragging pieces of wood on to the terraces, strange shapes; they said they were preparing for a party, that soon she would see merry-go-rounds and triumphal arches on the lawns, strange animals coming down the avenues. They talked about the feasts of Il Magnifico in Florence and of Il Moro in Milan, the people who paraded in the streets in their thousands coming forward with tiny steps on horses caparisoned in silks, copses of greenery where the masters let out lions or, for interminable sallies before the crowd, the mares and stallions from their stables. They talked of the great Palio. Gods and nymphs emerging from chariots, in the last rays of sunlight walking towards the triumphal arches.

Weary (at times he felt the approach of death), old and without sadness he made angels so beautiful they disturbed the senses, they beat their wings above the yew trees then fell gently back on to the grass of the flower-beds. Peaceful, in the evening he sat down near her and closed his eyes, he collected the last of his strength, for something that would have ceased to exist by the following day, working on it as he worked on the most ambitious artistic enterprise. What difference did it make? At Santa Maria delle Grazie he had studied the most scientific rules of perspective, geometry and the proportions of the human body, arranged in groups of three the apostles, greenish blues, wonderful ochres, their faces so handsome he no longer knew how he would depict Christ. When ambassadors and cardinals came to watch him paint they saw his hand shaking, they testified in their letters to his febrile genius: the master made such beautiful horses, such handsome apostles around Christ, the work would be one of the glories of Italy, months and months of labour. Yes, up there beneath church arches he shook on his scaffolding, in the evening in the morning, with exhaustion, with fear or anguish, he shook until the very last day. Then, once completed, more than completed, the work grew pale, lost its lines and colours, Christ and the apostles faded in the dusty chalk and the bitter clamminess of the walls. John, James, Simon and Judas, the same vague complexions, the same lost expressions, the same end to things; nothing would remain but the washed-out colours and the dull eyes, more than dead, of vague silhouettes as ghostly as the ones exhumed from ancient cities buried under rubble.

Shortly before February the cold lost its keenness. He asked for the horses to be saddled and they set off along the river. They walked slowly, leading the horses by the reins. The nettles gleamed under the ice, iridescent, pebble-smooth, and water creaked in the ruts, the river foamed around the bridge; further along, silent and hurried, it rolled the last of the ice, brown as the sky behind the trees. Brown too were the river and the sky, so low on those days that it was impossible to tell where one began and the other ended. All they could see when they looked from over by Montlouis was a kind of fog, an extension of the river, a thick veil all the way to the heights. Nothing was moving now but the river running towards the sea, the whole country lay beneath the grey and brown light, there was a mildness, a peace, unhappiness seemed to have been delayed.

They stopped, looked at the river, talked about the winters in Lombardy. Sometimes they looked at each other in silence, and then he asked them to move on; they took the bridge where, if they were heading westwards, they crossed the river on the ferryman's *futreau* and returned by the cliffs. Beneath the fog when they lifted their heads they could see a lightness, a pallor. When they arrived they walked on the path in front of the house, they said to themselves that she was waiting.

On the hillsides the light grew pale, veined with grey day after day, the wine-growers pruned the vines, they worked for another whole month, studied the props, the equipment, the lion-run and the course for the horses, the angels' faces and hair. The chariots, the gods and the nymphs.

~

All morning with the women of the castle she had been smearing the pigs with lard, covering them with herbs and stock, adding the verjuice and saffron and then putting them to roast in the ovens. Now, while the dragons dashed out on the terraces, and the long white angels by the plane trees, she served melons and Arbois wines, *clairets* from Orléans, marzipan, almonds and pine-nuts, quince pastes. In the avenues the women rustled with taffetas and silks, the cheekbones beneath the paint had a furtive, splendid brilliance; on the cushions of the bedizened wagons they outdid one another in singing and playing the lute, then all evening surrounded by their dogs and their parrots, diamonds at their breasts and pearls on gold thread, they entertained in their houses. Later the mildness of night entered the bedchambers and they ran so wild they thought they would die.

She had no need to say what she thought; he looked at the backs she turned to him, the stubborn napes beneath her coif, imagined dazzlement, bitter confusion. He understood; weary he looked at her and asked only to agree. To what, neither of them, not even she, could have said. When she climbed up to the top of the cliff she looked at the Loire flowing towards Angers, she looked at St Denis and St Hubert, the plains along the river, to the west they flowed towards Chinon, Loches to the south. She looked at the town and the forests, the river disappearing towards the sea.

What would remain of him and what in the end was eternity – and why all of a sudden was everything different from what she had known till then, and not different in fact but more like its opposite, like a glove turned inside out? One evening at nightfall she noticed him in the cellar, the next day at dawn when she got up he was still there. He had just glued the wings of a fly with honey; he wanted, he said, to observe its movements and the noises it made.

She watched the sun rise and heard the donkey braying over by the priory. One thing was the rain, the blue of the sky or the wind in the great trees; another, she said one evening, was the unhappiness behind walls.

*O*nce again summer promised to be warm and dry. Her feet bare in the boots he had given her she washed the ground with a great deal of water, went to the well and came back, crossed the yard with the buckets she emptied on the tiles; later on her knees by the puddles she brushed, scraped, scoured, when unsteady and half-dazed she stood up, she pushed back with her wrist a curl that had fallen on her temple, or with both hands her face and throat tilted up she clutched the small of her back, interminably drawing breath; a moment later she set off to fill the buckets and vanished into the lower rooms, the upper storeys or the cellar, and when he remarked that there was no need to rub, sweep or scour so much she asked how she could have done otherwise: with all their comings and goings in the dust of the terraces and the flies and ants coming back from everywhere imaginable, the house was dirtier than a stable floor.

They began to wait for the rain. The season was dry, one of those seasons that presaged bad heat to come, and the earth in the paths cracked, narrow, deep fissures like wounds. The sun turned the fields yellow; soon the rye and wheat would burn, it was a wretched year. She talked of the small workmen and the day-labourers, the miseries of the day.

They set off for Romorantin. Judging by what they were saying over there nothing was coming along or progressing as it should: the stone-cutters weren't ready, nor were the loggers or half of the masons, the men who brought the bricks, the plaster and the sand from Nousan and La Ferté; they were starting to say that the workers were falling ill, unexplained fevers they didn't even know the names of, and that the castle would never be finished. The journey took longer than expected, they were getting close to St John's Day and its fairs, the roads were clogged with mules and carts, pedlars and Egyptians telling fortunes and selling talismans; barriers and wine fountains were being set up all over the place. They collected flowers and dry herbs for the fires, on several occasions they avoided the main roads and took off across the wood; they slept in Pont-Levoy, came back via Montrichard and Gué-Péan. In the evening from the inns they saw the fires shining on the hillsides, in the church squares they heard voices and laughter, people drinking and dancing late into the night.

She stayed alone with the Italian manservant, did a great deal of washing and arranged the chests and wardrobes, he cleared the pond, tidied up the copse, repaired the pots in the garden and the planks of the bridge over the river, then he left. The manservant went to Blois in search of orange trees for the terraces and when he came back he stopped in Chaumont where, on the master's orders, he inquired about vines trained on pergolas, and the hardness of the stone for columns he had been asked to set up at the top end of an avenue.

They came back in the last days of July, made weary by the heat and the dust of the roads; it was a Saturday and the afternoon was drawing to a close, the river gleamed immobile beneath a light and transparent mist that moved in shades of gold, a calm, a peace at the day's end.

The pupils watered the horses and loosened their girths, walked them for a while before bringing them back, he crossed the terraces and came to greet her, to sit beside her for a few moments. He was the first to enter the kitchen. He was the first to see him.

Sitting on the stool, he was smiling in silence; he smiled all evening. Sometimes he groaned gently and looked at her. He was ageless, that was what he thought as he looked at them, sitting side by side with their backs to the chimney. She said she could not have done otherwise and that she would explain later. That was all. Evening fell. A red circle, looking almost distended, the sun touched the cliff-tops, then it bathed the depths of the park in a light that they looked at for a long time. The evening smelled of hot grass and boxwood. They said nothing for the rest of the time, even avoiding each other's eyes. They stayed silent till dusk.

When the first star appeared above Notre Dame des Grèves she said, in a loud and intelligible voice, as though she had gone a long way to get her breath, deciding to finish her phrase in a single desperate, endless exhalation, she said she apologized for the worry and it wouldn't last, she promised.

Then her voice broke, leading unexpectedly into silence. They looked at one another and fell silent again; leaving her with him they went up to the bedchambers.

~

They got used to his presence and asked no questions. To think that she had given them the habit of silence and things that must not be said. He did not once look at them and stayed aloof, groaning gently as he rocked on his stool. They got used to the moaning, the groans of a wounded animal. In the morning when they came down he was sitting beside her eating soup or oatmeal pap. Later she took him to the garden or to the shopkeepers of Bout-des-Ponts. On Sunday they went to the island, they watched the boys diving into the river or racing horses; the men called from one shore to another, they heard the voices, the laughter growing louder as the day declined. Before going back up she took him to pray at St John's chapel. He walked with a heavy tread and his shoulders low, his neck stretched forward, staring at the ground; sometimes he stood upright and emitted little cries as he looked at the sky. She showed him the birds on the river, the cranes and the cormorants, the rows of gulls on the sand-banks. Sometimes she only looked at him, sitting down she looked at him as though she had never seen him before, at other times she seemed to forget, she looked elsewhere or closed her eyes. He must have come from some hospice or some hovel at the end of a village where someone had looked after him until they couldn't do it any more and they told her, when perhaps she had stopped thinking about it long before, or rather found it too painful to think about, as we sometimes set aside things that are too painful and that way we manage to live. One evening she said that in other times, long ago, her mother had married her to the madder-dyer in Thésée, further down towards the other river beyond the forest. The dyer had given her a son and then fallen ill, he died of a bad fever, bad work in the clammy atmosphere of the vats. She said nothing more during all the days that followed. In the evening she would take him to see the donkey in the meadow, at the end of the park down by the little wood, then he went there on his own, each evening at the same time he went to get the donkey from the last paddock. From up there on the terrace she watched the two of them, then settled on a bench with her work; sometimes she could not see him and called to him, shouted after him to find out where he was, she would rise to her feet and, leaning on the edge of the avenue, try to spot him in the copse. Just past the columns he reappeared, he turned towards her and laughed loudly, opened the barrier and walked towards the donkey, ran, jumped, sometimes he stopped and laughed again, then he stayed there for a long time standing by the donkey, while they saw her from the studio windows sitting on her bench surveying the meadow. Not once did she raise her eyes towards the windows but she knew they were there watching her, watching her and him down there with the donkey in the meadow, and she knew what they were thinking. When he came back up she wiped his calves, the sandals soaked by the grass of the meadow; he sat down by the fire and watched the flames; sitting beside him she crossed her hands in her skirts, turned towards the terraces, towards the sun disappearing behind the cliffs.

*S*he became more silent than ever, and her silence and averted glances said more than words would have done, they spoke of habit and resignation; within her there spoke everyone who sat silently by the windows and crossed their hands in their skirts, just as within him, whom she watched with a tired eye, there lived all the idiots. All they saw was a pitiful, wretched fragment of time, without beginning or end, for a long time before and a long time to come people like themselves would linger in a street or a garden to watch an old donkey or an idiot, as they watched them saying to themselves that they were watching a donkey and an idiot of all the ages, changeless and eternal as the sky and the sun, the terrifying depths of the earth, unhappiness, happiness. As she, the one he watched, was the servant, all servants since the world had existed, since time had been endless, time would never end and life was so short.

That was what she said in the evening by the windows. Sometimes they saw her trembling and thought it was the cold. Without saying a word she told the whole story. One day the unhappiness had been so intense that it had marked the blood of the older ones, they had passed it on from mother to daughter like their red or fair hair, the whiteness and scent of their skin. They were barely grown before they waited for it, as one waits for an illness or a pain foretold, washed, scoured, sweated their bitter sweat in their clothes stiff with dirt, ran till they were breathless after the cow lost in the wood or the drunken husband in someone else's bed; they gave birth, gave birth, buried without a word children who had died of bad milk or forest sickness, sometimes they died barely out of the womb. The women went to the wood to pray to Our Lady of Mercy to give them life for an instant, long enough to be baptized and not lost to hell. In the early morning, blessed or not, they buried them without another word; coming back to their own homes they sat down and crossed their hands on their knees. Crying or moaning they would calm down, or simply groan as the animals groaned, gently and in a faint voice, time for suffering to be less intensely felt, time to make a pact with it.

And when they thought of the ones who lifted

their skirts in the vines or elsewhere, they caught fevers from it and sometimes hatred; others prettier than themselves lay down and opened their thighs, expecting pleasure, nothing but pleasure or perhaps money and pleasure, or maybe happiness when the man took them in his arms, whispered mad things in their ears, words that sounded like love, the madness of love, mad love. That they might not be cold and might forget everything they drew the faded cloth of the bedcurtains, but in their dreams everything started over again; they dreamed they were carrying their bundle of firewood that they were cold and could never warm up; again they worked, they bled, had children, were ashamed, ashamed, so tired that waking they could barely put one foot in front of the other. On clear days they came valiantly back up the avenues and sometimes even smiled; the rest of the time, on bad days, when the sky lay heavy on the roofs for a whole season at a time, they sat down without a word and crossed their hands in their knees.

As for them, what they heard was the mute, broken voice, the silent lament. They finally understood, they said nothing and looked at her, became aware of those things around them that were sliding imperceptibly into place, they thought about destinies, well-potted paths.

*B*y the time she took him away they had already stopped watching him. Barely a month had passed; as briefly as she had commented on his arrival among them she informed them that he was going to leave.

It was the evening the donkey died, the evening they found them by the back gate, the donkey and him, lying pressed one against the other. Clinging to the donkey's neck he was looking at it, looking at its eyes, the gaze of the donkey lying on its flank foaming its last drool. The donkey foamed with its eyes wide open and groaning gently; they heard the two breaths, the heavy, painful breath of the dying donkey and just as heavy and painful the breath of the idiot clinging to its neck; they heard the cries he sometimes uttered near the animal, sometimes he wept, sometimes he shouted, and the shout rose to bursting, to slide noisy and wet like a cloud bursting over the roofs, a ship sinking suddenly to unimagined depths. They watched the two of them all the time that the donkey took to die.

Throughout all that time she too wept in the meadow, aloof beneath the green oaks, wept in silence, then when the donkey had died, night was already falling, she went and took him by the hand and led him to the kitchen. Later they climbed the stairs to the attic. They barely heard them. Yes, it was this evening, she said, that he would be leaving.

It was so hot over the next few days that they thought the mildness would not come back or the clouds or the wind that rose from the shores in the evening. Between Nevers and Angers the river dried up, lingered on the sands, dried away in a very pale, almost white light, the ponds flickered between the bushes. Further up towards Vendôme the peasants had gone to see the priest to ask him to make rain, a whole month evening and morning they had knelt before God, walking in the streets and holding processions.

They had to keep reserves of water, she said the well could run dry. Standing against the coping she filled the buckets and took them down to the cellar, she must have been praying, they saw her lips moving, her murmur reached them monotonous as a litany. The dogs groaned lying at the bottom of the walls, they stayed in the twilight. For a whole week they could not find sleep and went late to bed; in the evening he set off with his horse and came back only at the first light of dawn, all night wandering in the cliff-top woods with his horse and further down on the seamen's path. When he came back he slept, then withdrew to the studio; no one knew what he was doing, neither the pupils nor the manservant. On the tables among the anatomical studies they laid out the plans for the castle, the great staircase and the colonnades, the past year's labours, the drawings he picked up one by one and studied as he would have studied someone else's work; he had stopped working. They talked about it, they said the great heat was exhausting them, that they would have to wait, everything was bound to get better soon, he heard them; he barely replied, he let them go on talking as he let the time pass, the days sometimes so long now that he ended up thinking about her. He looked at her. She washed the bedchambers and the sheets and everything there was to be washed and got rid of amid the smells of soap and the lavender that she threw in great fistfuls on the floors, pushing back to their furthermost reaches the dirt and stains and doubtless the moment of thinking and suffering, pushing away with all her final unbelievable strength her suffering, ignoring it as with courage and obstinacy one ignores something of which one disapproves. He said to himself that she had brought that other one here to show him, the idiot, the timeless child, as others might have shown their illnesses, their cankers or their injuries, she had shown her son, had displayed him as one might display a bad scar, a leper's hand, so that he understood from her what there was to understand, with courage and madness and her eyes closed waiting for the revelation, the astonishment to pass.

He looked at her, forgot his notebooks, without even looking at her he noted her gestures, her movements; back in his room he remembered her moving near him, hasty and silent amid the muffled sound of fabrics, watching her coming and going around him in her grey canvas dresses, without a thought carrying out her everyday movements, calmly and without giving up her work waiting for the death that was coming. He wondered if anything of any importance was left. When she came back up from the river with her baskets she sat down for a moment by the back gate, her legs were shaking and she was short of breath; slowly she got back on her feet and came up the rest of the path, soon appeared in the doorway and smiled, straight as anything and had never behaved any other way. Peacefully she came to sit next to him; yes, perhaps all that remained would be the moment when he noticed her coming back up the avenue and soon after that the one when she appeared smiling and sad at the door, her features drawn with weariness and the heat of the afternoon, all that remained of everything he had ever seen would be that image of the little woman whose frail silhouette was outlined against the light of the terraces and who no longer seemed affected by anything. He could say to himself that he had no regrets and had nothing to regret, he did not know why and did not try to know, at once forgetting and remembering – not forgetting, really, but letting himself be lulled, numbed by the sweet, sad idea, the peaceful habit, the woman who near him and in silence buried her sadness and bitterness beneath the patient repetition of everyday gestures, the stubborn assertion that everything would continue, the sun rose and fell, the sky was blue, the sky was grey, they were gathered there under a single roof as if on a boat battling a hostile sea, always wondering which of life and death would win. He let himself be lulled as he would have let himself be lulled by the summer wind or one of those gentle and mysterious voices from childhood. Time passed. At one moment or another she raised her eyes and looked at him, she now seemed to be seeking his eye, sometimes went so far as to attract it by being provocative and clumsy; he observed the challenge and the clumsiness, the confusion, he understood that nothing would be as before and that that was good; she asked if he wanted her to light the fires they had allowed to go out or if it wasn't worth it, or even if he planned to leave the next day, and if he did where would he go. While she talked he looked at the transparent grapes in a basket or a fly ceaselessly walking down and climbing back up a sun-warmed pane of glass; in the end he told himself she had always been there, sometimes it was even as though he was remembering her carrying him along in each of her steps and the great sweep of her skirts. He thought of childhood in the hills, remembered the long blue skirts and light sandals on a brown leg, imagined the happiness that might still be and a final gentleness, murmurs and arms wrapped around him, told himself that time was not important, never would be, no matter what else might happen. He watched her, forgot, realized he was forgetting, love too mad and the child gone for ever, the first and last embraces and the great frescoes that would not survive him, day after day eroding in the bitter clamminess of the churches, finished, unfinished, the work that would die with him; everything would vanish of love and desire and days to make the world anew, everything but the drawings and the sketches and the three paintings he had brought all the way here. The end was coming for him and for her, what was left for them really to think of, to desire as one desires a haven, or the joy of those first dreams, and what had they ever desired but the days that would come and could do nothing but come; yes, what difference was there now between their lives? They would die offered up and con-senting, they would leave without memory or regret. He imagined her by his side on the last day, standing half hidden by the bedcurtains, her hands on the fold of her skirts and her face in the shadow of her coif, the only gleam a cheekbone in the faint light that entered the room at that time of day, and maybe the rim of her lip where the flesh still gently swelled; silent and motionless she would watch him die. He imagined her in the early hours, her features drawn and her transparent lids blue with weariness, mute and motionless, bolt upright in her grey dress, she would watch him die in the pale morning. It was as though she understood, sitting opposite him on the stool, barely shrunken with weariness, she looked at him, the sun lit her cheek and temple, her eye gleamed in the light rising from the terraces, the day was coming to an end, all the days of that endless summer, the last, he thought. Most often they looked at each other in silence, they barely understood one another when they spoke. When she was slow to smile, he wondered why.

The days drew in. At four o'clock she lit the candles, he picked up papers and pencils and started drawing as before, when his hand shook he watched it shake and then put it on the table, observed his hand, the void and the silence, the weariness that descended at the same time each evening. They talked about his shaking hand, and about the drawings that were always the same; he heard them, the pupils and the servant and the ones who still came to see him, who took their seats around him by the fireplace, speaking of Italy, saying that now the wars were over people were turning against the Turk and how the Pope in person, barefoot in the streets, was exhorting the princes to join against him. He looked at the three paintings, the anatomical studies or, again, the stairs of the great castle; he admired, remembered, talked about the work, he listened to them, nodded his acquiescence to their suggestions; they were talking not about him but about someone else he still remembered. When she arrived he asked her to serve them mulled wine or eggnog, they would be leaving soon, they didn't want to tire him any longer, they said. It was only later when they passed through the arch and moved away along the cliff road on their horses that he felt fatigue and sadness crashing down upon him like a bad fever. He talked about sadness and fatigue, or perhaps about something that resembled sadness and fatigue. Mere loneliness, at once bitter and sweet.

Death was coming, not what he feared most, that was his shrinking movements and his body which was no longer as it had been, it was the coming night, long and sleepless. He wanted days without night and light in the sky to the very end. He went to bed late then once upstairs he came back down again, lit lamps and candles, dragged his chair across the floor and sat down by the still-burning fire; he poked the logs, moved pails and andirons, making so much noise that at last she came down, saying she had heard him and asking him if he needed anything. She crossed the woollen fichu over her breast and two pale plaits framed her cheeks; he looked at her in the light of the candle that she held in her hand before she put it down to look in a chest for something she could give him to eat and drink. After giving it to him she lingered for a moment, asking if he was sure he didn't need anything, put a log back in the fireplace, poked the fire for a moment longer, went to check if the doors were properly closed and then went back upstairs.

Between the declining summer and the fullness of autumn there were several nights like that, time for winter to come, time for him to get used to the long nights, the cold and sadness of the season.

She said the cranes were flying low and winter would be tough, that she had seen the castle guards shooting birds with blunderbusses on the cliffs, then roasting them on stones. She put a little pot of pears on the fire, said that in town they had whipped two men who had been begging by the church of St Denis; she talked about the thieves and rogues, and the ones in chains who cleared the drains and dug ditches, the ones who had had an ear cut off for stealing; the season was hard, some had already died at the foot of the walls. He was listening, melting little pearls from Milan in the juice of a lemon, making a paste of them and with a twist moulding them to the size of a fingernail, polishing them with a piece of chalcedony and threading them on a gold chain.

When she returned from nones he gave her the pearl necklace. She put it on and thanked him, then went down to the garden to fetch some herbs. Once past the back gate she stopped and turned round, looking towards the kitchen. When she came back she said it was starting to rain, a warm rain that had started over the slopes. They watched the rain falling in great warm drops; she talked about the coming winter. She thanked him again for the pearl necklace and then went upstairs to bed.

She had arrived via the terraces; he remembered the rubbing of slippers on stone and the cold air when she had pushed the door. She must have hesitated for a moment then he had noticed the face that she poked through the doorway before coming in. He had not left the kitchen that evening, he had not even gone upstairs and come back down as he sometimes did lately, he had said he would stay for a little while, and he was not sleepy. He would not be long, he had added. And then he must have gone to sleep by the fire, unable to move and watching the flames he must have dozed off. When the door had creaked he had given a start and felt the cold air, he had opened his eyes and seen her, motionless, hesitating in the doorway as though on the threshold of a strange house. He had not understood why, now that she had come downstairs and woken him, she stayed there without moving and did not put any sticks on the fire or blow it, nor did she ask him what he needed and why he had not gone to bed. She had said nothing when he had stayed downstairs, she herself had barely lingered, barely tarried before going upstairs; she had bidden him goodnight and returned to her garret as she did on other evenings. He had heard the last sounds in the bed-chambers and then nothing more; he remembered the silence in the house, the time that had passed before he went to sleep. The moon still lit the ter-races but could no longer be seen from the kitchen, the moonlight must have been shining on the little wood; he said to himself that she must have been waiting all the time she was up there, listening out for sounds in the house and the moment when he would go upstairs to bed, saying to herself that she had to go downstairs, that if she didn't speak that night she would never speak. Perhaps even by dint of waiting and hesitating she in turn had fallen asleep, and when later she had woken she had remembered, had known from the windows, still lit, that he had not left the kitchen and that she had to go and see him, then she had come out of her room along the first-floor gallery and then down via the watchtower; she had seen the light from the windows below trembling on the ground between the shadow of the yews and the shadow of the little box trees around the pillars. There was still an hour, perhaps two, before daybreak.

She had appeared before him quite upright, quite frail in her night-dress, so frail he had said to himself, almost invisible among all the thick cloth, that apart from her face and neck which emerged from her respectably fastened collar it would have been easy to forget that there was a body beneath the dress, albeit an old woman's body, thin and weary. There were no suggestions of it, the dress looked as though it had been placed starched on the floor, its astonishing brilliance, the matt whiteness of the well-worn.

She asked him to excuse her and said she had no wish to disturb him, but like himself she could not get to sleep. Also, since a certain amount of time had passed, she wanted to ask him something, or rather inform him how things stood on a subject that concerned him; she had taken the liberty to come and discuss it with him. She had not talked about it to anyone, neither the pupils nor the servant; he would understand and keep it to himself, she begged him, as she begged him to forgive her frankness and perhaps also her indiscretion, for perhaps it was indiscreet to talk this way.

Tired as she was, it was not impossible that she

would be the first to go; she did not say it by way of complaint, or to impose upon him in any way, she was not unhappy here, as far as that was concerned she had no regrets, but nothing was as it had been, he must know that. In the evening when she went to bed and in the morning when she got up when weariness hit her she felt a pain in her chest, and her legs would not support her; to tell the truth she saw the point approaching when she would no longer be able to serve him. It wasn't easy for her to talk like this, to tell herself that she was going to disappoint him, she hoped he would understand.

As she was talking the smells of quenched fires and old stone reached them and, from the other side of the wood with the wind, the stench of damp earth. The rains must have come via Nantes and Angers, within two days they would be here with the morning mists. At five o'clock in the evening the darkness would rise from the land, opaque, grey and close; summer had been so hot and the heat had hastened the end of things. It was an odd year, the sadness had been there since before the autumn. Day would soon be breaking, pale and grey, and towards the horizon sometimes there would still be the brilliance of a mild season, warmth, a kind of respite. He too was tired and he knew what she meant, but knew too that it was not for him to talk about it that she had come to see him. He looked at her, as he had done every day since they had been there. What else had he been doing all that time, and what else was he thinking about at that precise moment, what else could he think about now that she was there, exposed and powerless, and stronger, a thousand times stronger than he in the face of what was to come? What she had to say she had not yet said, but he knew it would not be a surprise (and even before she spoke he knew that as long as he lived he would remember, that every day he would have before his eyes the image of the little woman in her white dress, putting her whole body, her whole thought, into a single great effort to say what she had to say, courageously, stopping then starting again, carrying on, while she still held the candle she had lit to come down, her face and eyelids hollowed by the trembling light, insomnia. Lower down on her cheek, clasping her lips, he saw the thick shadow of fatigue).

Now there was something else she wanted to say. It was harder but perhaps he might understand it, for it was not wild talk or madness or presumption, but something she had been thinking about for a long time. She was an old woman and his servant, and it was with a view to being useful that she had come to see him. She spoke in short sentences, breathless; she stopped, took a long draught of air, naked, invisible in the thickness of the cloth, motionless against the door, she had barely moved a step since coming in, intimidated like a stranger entering a strange house. In a single breath as though unwinding the last length of a skein and closing her eyes she said the rest.

It was just in case he needed her again, after-wards, later on, she said. When she was no longer there. Yes, when she was dead, she went on, and her voice grew assertive, when she was dead perhaps once more, one last time, she could be of some use to him. She moved, imperceptibly; she must have moved a leg forward, or wanted to, under the thick fabric of her dress, the same thick, heavy material she had used to make blankets for them and dustcloths; she must have wanted to move forwards towards the middle of the kitchen, towards her own place near the table where she prepared and served their meals. It was as though beneath the ample austerity of the night-dress movement gradually resumed as now she looked into his eyes. She was his servant, she said, devoted to the very end, she knew how interested he was in his studies and she had seen the drawings and knew what they were about, she thought that, well, recently she'd been saying to herself that once she was dead she might be more use than she had been alive, maybe he would still need her then, that was what she wanted to say.

She walked, pressing the fabric of her blouse to herself with both hands, coming and going across the kitchen, talking, talking; had she in all her born days ever had to utter so many words? He thought she wouldn't be able to stop, she could continue on that trajectory that night and all the nights to come, she had been silent too long, she would talk herself to death, she would die of talking, there in front of him in that kitchen which was her home, with its light brick walls and the windows from which she contemplated the cliffs at evening, and yet when she talked it was as though the silence were continuing, as though she were tending with all her strength towards silence, towards darkness, towards that place, that time, when she would once again be alone, unknown, calmly despairing.

And was he not already giving her an answer? By saying nothing, by merely looking at her, was he not acceding to her request, this entreaty whose idea had come to her evening after evening in her garret, she who had never asked for anything, not fabric for her dresses nor a woollen cloth coat, nor a single day off apart from Sundays and feast days, or anything else; he said nothing, could say nothing, he watched her coming and going across the kitchen, wondered when and how the idea had come to her, and then once the idea had come, at what moment it had occurred to her to talk to him about it, how day after day, night after night, the idea had taken its course, until this day, this night, when she had had the courage to come downstairs and then once she had come downstairs, to take it to its conclusion, to talk, to confide the idea, the unbelievable request, just as sometimes – and already life is almost over – with one final effort we throw off something that has grown too heavy. Yes, when and how had she conceived and then nurtured the idea, which evening, which morning had she said to herself that she would come and get him and talk to him as she was doing now? He remembered those movements towards him, rapidly deflected, like the looks that would suddenly flow from between her eyelids, the silences that followed, the bitter need to say nothing.

She came towards her stool and sat down in her usual place. The fire had gone out and he could barely see her now, all that emerged from the shadows was the white dress and sometimes when she turned towards him a cheekbone or the tip of a plait, the kind of pale, almost mother-of-pearl curl that her hair made when it escaped from her coif. She crossed her hands on her knees. He rediscovered her, recognized her and what she thought she had never needed to say, neither astonishment nor confusion nor even disapproval, now it was as though he was thinking it in his turn, as though it had come from far away, as though the tortured idea that had appeared one evening in the old woman's life had made its way to him. He thought of the corpses in the hospices of Rome and Milan, the open bellies, the drawings scattered about on the tables, filled notebooks and great folios, naked men on tables penetrating invisible women, pale-eyed men with glorious members penetrating women with invisible faces, all that was shown was the bellies and the penetrated, fertilized wombs, invisible women endlessly penetrated. He imagined her preparing to die, washing herself, doing her hair, putting on her best night-dress, the least drab, the least worn, the one whose folds would be best set off by starch, dressing herself up as she would have dressed herself up for a wedding; he imagined her exposed, yielding, he thought of submission. Yes, if she died, if she were now to pass on in the midst of them, and yes, of course that was what he wanted, he could do as he took her to mean, do with her as he had done with the others, the ones she resembled, he knew that.

Near the stables they heard the little owl, then behind the sheds a dog barked. Over at Artigny by the last poplars the sky grew pale and the wind rose, chasing the leaves across the terraces. The morning was going to be clear, without clouds or mist, a clear November morning. He looked at her, he saw her at the end of the meadow with the donkey and the idiot, and coming back up the avenues on clear mornings, the next day turning her back on them amid her clatter of ironwork and pots, ignoring them for days on end then in the rustle of her skirts coming towards him and with the sweetest of smiles holding out to him a cooked apple or a glass of *clairet*.

For was she not like them (she looked at him, would not stop looking at him, even when she drew breath and stopped talking she still went on looking at him)? Was she not like the ones he had opened up in the depths of cellars and contemplated for whole nights at a time, old men, children or women who had died in childbirth, the ones who had died homeless, without roof or shelter and with no one to come and claim them, no one who ever would, a stranger to everyone, delivered to the loneliness of the hospices and then of the cemeteries, submitting for the last time and with no more importance than cows drowned in ditches when the ponds burst? Did they not have that in common, that was what she meant, those people and she herself, who served him right here in the house, who knew no one and had never known anyone, who had only known other people's lives, had seen other people living and loving, seducing, weeping. Every day she had washed, in their name she had cleaned the marks of life and shamelessly stained linen, at night she had heard them dying in the arms of others and being by day reborn in dazzling brocades, then waiting once again for looks and caresses and the words that might keep them till evening where beneath the bedcurtains all of life and death would start over once again. She who for other reasons awaited death, stupor, and deep sleep. Saw them without even looking. Knew everything there was to know of them and their stories. She was giving her body, yielding it up. One last time he would be able to study how a woman who had suffered, who was ageing, was made; a woman used to expecting and hoping for nothing but the end of things and who by dint of turning over and over the same sad and weighty memories did not even fear death. He would pay no attention to weariness and old age, he would see her wretched with her hair undone, in the light of the candles burning till morning as they burned that night in the kitchen. There would be no need to pay attention to her. Who would have done her hair after all and prepared her as the dead are prepared? Yes, she said, what business had she rotting in a graveyard? What she said was not a blasphemy and God would understand. Then, when she had stopped talking, when she had said the final word and knew that no one else would come, could come, gently she began to weep.

They said nothing; they said nothing for a long time. When he turned towards the window he saw the white sky beyond the terraces; she was sitting on her stool, head bowed. She had not moved but he perceived a movement, something emanating from her, with a barely perceptible rustling, shifting the air around them. Her heart must be beating wildly, one last feeling, one word yet to be said and which would not be said. Then the space closed back over them like water over the bows of the flat-bottomed boats that sailed down the river. The immobility and thickness of the silence. Nothing moved now, not a creak or a rustle. A cat lifted its head then went back to sleep, its jaw stretched out all along one paw. For a moment a cloud revealed the sun, a light, neither gold nor grey, penetrated the kitchen and touched the wood of the table and the floor around them; further off a cock crowed. He heard her breathing, calmly. She looked at the sky at the top of the windows, white and, over towards the west, light clouds fringed with darkness above the grey leaden masses soldered to the horizon. She stayed like that for a long time, and said it was going to rain. From the slopes the first sounds of the day came down, harnesses and the hoofs of the mules on the cliff road; life was resuming. She looked at him and smiled, asked him if he wanted his breakfast now.

*I*t rained every morning, every afternoon, for the whole of November, the sky bursting with pockets of water, muted downpours like the ones that swept the land in spring. It rained till Advent. The river swelled; she said it would take the island and the part of town called Bout-des-Ponts. They repaired the downpipes, plugged gaps and holes, the water ran over the walls, they sponged down the walls, the windows ran with condensation. They closed themselves in the corners of the rooms, heard the rain crashing on the roofs, and sometimes a kind of storm, a warm, heavy tempest from over by the Sologne. When the rain intensified they talked loudly, shouted and repeated things, then without saying another word they looked at each other, saying nothing until it was over. The dogs barked behind the doors. That was how winter came. The second and last winter.

Where appearances were concerned nothing

had changed; she came and went in the house, busy as ever, but more animated, clumsy and bumping into the chests and bedsteads as she strode too briskly around, catching her skirts on a door-handle and ripping them through. For a whole week she did not speak or even look at them. They saw her going around the hearth end-lessly poking it, spreading out the embers under the stewing-pots; in a kind of last, long rout she impatiently swept the table of peelings and empty glasses, went over it with a rag, put on the table-cloth. She must have been tired, and she must have found it hard to get to sleep; sitting by the fire she supped her curds and oatmeal pap, her features drawn and her eyelids grey, looking through the windows more than ever, looking outside, proclaiming silently and with all her strength that the world was elsewhere. He saw her again, standing against the door in her white dress, frail and upright and motionless for such a long time. He thought of the time remaining, wondering which of them would be the first to die. It was as though they were waiting, they didn't really know what for, but what they did know was that something was coming. The pupils said noth-ing, he said to himself that they understood.

When the rain stopped she went up on to the

cliff. Beyond the last houses they saw her taking the path, catching her breath on a rock or a tree-trunk; she stopped for a moment, looked at the grey roofs, the dark line of the forests further away towards Pont-Levoy, and on days when the west wind blew, the slate-boats of Trélazé going back up the river, grey-brown tartans, with great square sails like the caravels when they sailed with the wind behind them. She barely lingered there, they soon saw her coming back down again taking little steps, holding her hair with one hand, her skirts blown back by the wind. She stopped, one last time she looked at the river towards the sea. When she came back she went towards the fire-place, lifted a pot-lid, murmured something they couldn't hear, got out the table-cloth, put out the bowls, the water, the wine, the bread. Soon she served them.

By the porch one evening they saw a man on his mule. He was coming down from the cliffs and must have arrived via the slope, over by the first forests. He had stopped under the arch with his cap in his hand. Then they had seen Battista setting off for the kitchen and coming back with her. They had spoken for a moment, the man who seeing her had dismounted from his mule and she still wiping her hands on her apron, watching him, the man speaking, in a low voice telling her why he had come, then looking at the house, the terraces as though she had never seen them before. Watching the ones who crossed the yard and reached the bedchambers via the gallery, finally lowering her eyes as he took his leave, or rather dismissing him, letting him know that it was time for him to go back where he had come from. Thanking him for his trouble, and for taking such a long journey.

The next day the rain resumed; they heard the wind and the water smashing against the windows, the roaring in the chimney. She had crouched down in front of the fire and turned the spit, he saw her back and the weary nape of her neck, and the bottom of her skirts dragging in the ashes and the bark dust.

Without turning round she said she would have to go. That tomorrow, Monday, with his permission, she would leave. She wouldn't be long, it was a matter of a few days. She asked him only to give her time to go and come back, she would return in three days, maybe four, not more than that. She had, she repeated, cleaned the house and prepared food for the time she would be away, filled the cauldrons and the plates in the cellar, for dinner and supper they had only to heat them slowly on the remaining ashes, to get everything finished that morning she had kneaded and worked the flour and put the loaves in the oven. They couldn't remember hearing her going up to her garret; later when they thought about it they said to themselves that she hadn't slept, that she had spent the night in the kitchen and had only gone up there to pack her things hastily and go. Her son was dead, she said. She would be back as soon as she had buried him.

She hadn't wanted them to take her. Hadn't even said where she was going, once past the porch she had turned round and looked at them, they had heard matins ringing at Notre Dame des Grèves and St Denis, then they had seen her going off with her brown canvas bag, her old wool cape over her Sunday dress, the goat's fur hat and the boots he had given her. It was raining. Walking quickly along on little steps she had followed the slope, walked eastwards along the river; they didn't know where she was going, all they knew was that she was going towards the valleys. Not very far, she had said, and that she would be back in two days or three, four at the very most, the time it took to bury her son.

They waited for her. For the whole of December and the beginning of January. Then the cold returned, all of a sudden it seized hold of the countryside and the river, the sky turned blue, he looked at the sky, the clear blue of the winter sky.

One morning he called for his horse to be saddled and left. The river was running swift and transparent; motionless the gulls slipped on the current in tight groups, the white stone of a steeple gleamed in the sun. In the blue winter sky the horse trotted gently, beyond life, beyond death; on the opposite shore he saw a cart pulled by oxen and behind it a child on his donkey, still further away dogs chasing each other barking.

It was in February, a little before Lent, that they learned the news from the locksmith who spent the winter in the forest. He had met her on the Souvigny road. It was late one afternoon and it was cold, a north wind that had come up after the rain. He had noticed the weary gait, the dragging leg, the dog too, an elderly woman and a dog wasn't something you expected to see on the roads around here. They had talked, she had said she was heading towards the river and that she was making her way back to the master's house,

she had wanted to avoid the forest, she was afraid
of the forest and even small woods, she had said.
Then she had taken a whole detour via the valleys, she had done more walking than she should
have done, that's all she had said about herself,
and then she had talked about the dog; she didn't
know the dog and didn't know where it came
from, in the valleys after the last houses it had
started walking behind her, she had chased it
away in the evening but the next day it had come
back, it must have taken a shortcut through the
woods, it had caught up with her when she was
leaving the vineyards and had started walking
behind her again, first in the background, then
far away on the slope as though to make itself
invisible. She had kept it, what else could she do,
she said, they kept one another company. She
spoke slowly, in a low voice. Together in the
evening they stopped in barns and ate the bread
that she took from her pocket and soaked in the
milk they gave them after milking the cow; she
apologized for any embarrassment, she said, but
they wouldn't disturb anyone, they would be
gone at daybreak. They breathed the smell of the
farms, slept side by side in the straw or hay in the
barns, and at dawn they left, she in her old
woollen cape, frail, so frail that she was barely

visible in all the length of the folds, and he smelling his wet dog smells trotting endlessly behind her. When the locksmith had asked why she was making the whole journey on foot and not getting up on to one of the carts that were coming down towards the river she had said it wasn't the first time and she knew what walking was. She lowered her eyes as she spoke. He had noticed the fine leather boots, and the mud on the bottom of her skirts, her hands red with cold, chapped, the pearl necklace. At Artigny he had set off for the forest. She had said she would go and find the ferryman after the vines, she would ask him to take her down to the first cliffs, from there she had said she would walk along the river and would be at the master's house before night-fall.

The rest he had learned from the people in Artigny on his way back through. It was the dog, he said, that had attracted attention. It had started barking at around midnight and then continued; it had barked all night. They had heard the dog as far as the valleys and well beyond the vines towards the river, the dog howling at her in the blackest of night, the bitter cold, the dog barking death, and worse than death, the people from the farms had said. The strange dog she had fed every day since she had first met it and which for a whole long night, the last night, had looked after her on the vineyard slope, motionless, then circling round her, groaning, howling endlessly at the sky, the depths of the earth or the fearful forest, howling the night, howling death, while the rain had started falling in tight drops, bitter and cold, the rain of bad days, of bad ideas, when everything was over for ever.

They had come from the farms with their candles, they had looked at the woman dying on the bank in her cape and her wet boots whose sole, torn all the way across its length, revealed her skin, red, purple, bloated like leather, the fine leather boots he had given her the year before and which she had never taken off even in the great heat. They had watched her dying in her wet grey skirts, her hand on her pearl necklace, peaceful, discreet, that was what they had said to themselves, as if to the very end she had been worried about disturbing anyone. They even had the impression that she was smiling.

A fog rose from the river, cold, as penetrating as rain. At about five o'clock in the evening he developed a fever. He asked for his pelisse to put over his knees, or else for them to bring down a canvas bed, and stayed in the kitchen sweating out his fevers by the fire. He was looking out of the window when the fog lifted. He said the fog was lifting, he watched the sun lighting the cliffs then disappearing. He listened to the horses in the stable and further away on the slope the dogs barking. He saw big skirts in folds, and the shadow in the folds, and sometimes a light higher up on a bodice, an arm. More and more hands. Pale napes beneath the head-dress, a grey plait falling on to her back. He asked them to bring him paper, he was still trying to draw but his hand would not obey. He saw a pale-eyed angel kneeling by Christ in mottled folds, turning away and looking at something, someone out of view, the moist eye and gently swollen lids of children torn from sleep. Sometimes everything had been so magnificent and dying was no longer of any importance.

He asked them to call the notary, and shortly before April put his affairs in order. To his pupil Salai he gave the vines at Porta Vercellina given him by Sforza; to the pupil Melzi the notebooks and drawings, thousands of them. To Fanfoia the furniture in the houses at Empoli. To Battista the manservant the black woollen cloth coat. Death wasn't up to much; she talked about it every day as she sat by the windows. He said to himself that he would wait for the blue sky before dying. That soon the sky would be blue.

Baule, March 1996 – December 1997